MW00938620

the perfectly imperfect match

Suttonville
Sentinels

the perfectly imperfect match

Suttonville
Sentinels

KENDRA C. HIGHLEY

Entangled Publishing, LLC
2614 South Timberline Road
Suite 109
Fort Collins, CO 80525
Visit our website at www.entangledpublishing.com.

Crush is an imprint of Entangled Publishing, LLC.

Edited by Heather Howland
Cover design by Bree Archer
Cover art from Shutterstock

Manufactured in the United States of America

First Edition July 2017

For Ron Querry
For teaching me how to tell a story

Chapter One

DYLAN

Dylan Dennings wiped sweat from his forehead, listening to the chain link fence at the back of the ball field bang in a stiff westerly wind. Dust kicked up from the infield as he considered his opponent. He'd need to compensate for the wind, just a little. Calculate where he wanted the ball to go.

"Dude, for God's sake, throw it already!" Tristan Murrell called, waving his bat in annoyance. "I want to wrap this up before I'm too old to kiss my girl!"

His girl. Alyssa *was* Tristan's, no denying that. Dylan was happy for them, but it still stung to be riding the bench when it came to a girl he'd had a major crush on. On the other hand, he probably dodged a bullet. If he wanted to make it to the minors in twelve months, he couldn't waste energy on anything else.

He had to stick to The Plan.

Dylan eyed Tristan. His hitting had improved a ton, thanks to his girlfriend's coaching, and he'd become nearly impossible to strike out. Worse, since they'd been playing together for years, Tristan knew all of Dylan's pitches.

Except one.

He'd been working on splitters with his coach, and he wanted to try it on someone. Tristan would do. Dylan wound up, letting the ball settle in his left hand, then with one fluid motion, flung the ball hard with the tiniest downward flick. Hopefully the ball would drop, just a bit, right as it crossed the plate.

And drop it did. Tristan swung with all his might, and why not? He thought he was seeing a nice, fat fastball. But Tristan's bat whooshed over the ball, sending him stumbling off-balance. Awesome.

"When the hell did you learn to throw a splitter?" Tristan flashed him an astonished smile. "That's big league crap."

"I spent a few weeks with Coach Myers." Dylan shrugged. "The more I can do, the better I look to scouts."

"You're the only guy I know who'd spend the first month of summer vacation, *after* winning the state championship, working out a new pitch." Tristan shook his head. "You ever think you might be a little too intense for your own good? Seriously, you need some time off."

No such thing as too intense, not when your future was on the line. "I'll take time off once the Rangers or the 'Stros take a good hard look at me for their farm system. I want to be triple-A by the time I'm twenty. If I can do that, I should be called up before I'm twenty-three."

Tristan walked out to the mound, carrying his bat with him. "I get it, and making it as a pitcher is even harder, but you're missing out on the fun stuff. Come to the lake with Alyssa and me tonight."

Dylan's heart sank, just a bit. *Yeah, because being a third wheel is so great. Not.* "Camp starts day after tomorrow." He waved a hand at the Suttonville High baseball field. "I told

Coach I'd make sure everything was set."

Tristan sighed. "It *is* set. We've been working on this for days. It's two weeks with a bunch of fourth and fifth graders... there's not much else to do here. Come with us. Live a little."

"I'd be a third wheel, and you know it." Dylan gave his friend a tight smile. "Besides, my mom wants us to go out to dinner tonight 'as a family' so I can't bail."

"Doesn't that sound like fun?" Tristan turned to go, but stopped. "I really wish you'd come with."

"I'm fine, seriously. Go on." Dylan waved him off. "I'll see you at eight tomorrow. Don't forget."

"Yes, boss."

Tristan disappeared through the locker room door, and Dylan let himself relax. Going out with Tristan and Alyssa wasn't bad, but Alyssa always wanted to fix him up with someone, maybe as a consolation.

"With that blond hair and blue eyes, you look like a surf board commercial," she would say. "There are two dozen girls who'd hit that. Let me introduce you. *Please.* There's this one girl who was in Algebra II with me last year who—"

And Dylan would always tell her no. He'd felt so out of control during the playoffs, and he couldn't afford that again. No distractions, no drama, no girls. Nothing but focus, avoiding blisters, and hard, hard work. That was what his senior year would have to look like: clean living and discipline.

He could have fun after he made the majors. Hell, by then girls would be falling into his lap at every turn. A star pitcher for the majors would have his pick.

Dylan finished tidying up the dugout, checked the foul lines for any smudged chalk, and made sure the water coolers were clean. By the time he was done, Coach had walked into the locker room, eyebrow raised. "Dennings, you should be long gone by now. Is there a problem?"

"No, sir. I'm just double checking everything and making

sure it's perfect. We want these kids to stick with the sport and win you another championship, right?"

Coach grunted, but Dylan could tell he was pleased. "I appreciate it. Now go home and get some rest. Three hours a day with those kids will wear you out quicker than sprint drills."

"I hear you, sir. See you Monday."

Dylan went to the parking lot, feet dragging. It's not that he didn't want to go home—home was fine. He just felt like there was more to do here. There was *always* more to do. Still, protecting his arm had to be a priority, and pulling his shoulder dragging equipment around would suck. So much was riding on this clinic, though. Being able to teach and coach would prove he had what it took. So what if his fastball was ninety miles per hour?

He needed *confidence*.

Most pitchers had a diva complex—he'd heard that from everyone, including Tristan—but did they have soul-crushing doubt before games? Probably not. He liked to win, and he didn't like quitting, but it was so hard to power through sometimes. Teaching the little guys, showing them how to throw, seemed like a great way to prove to himself that he knew what he was doing and to stop freaking out over every minute detail.

Hopefully it worked.

And if it didn't? If it didn't…he couldn't think about that. Not yet. He couldn't think about his parents, knowing they secretly hoped he'd go on to college. He wouldn't think about blowing it in front of scouts next season.

His breath hitched and his pulse sped up. A bead of sweat ran down his temple. Dylan started his car—a Porsche crossover handed down from his mom—and turned on the A/C. *Calm down, asshole. You're fine.*

But the little voice in his head kept telling him he wasn't good enough…and he had no idea how to shut it off.

Chapter Two

"Who made *this*?" The girl in the front of the shop sounded impressed. "Come look!"

"A corset? With…what are those? Clockwork bats?" The other girl sounded less impressed. "Seriously, those are *bats.*"

"I want it," the first girl said. "It's so…so…*me.*"

The second girl laughed. "Well, that's kind of true."

As their footsteps approached, Lucy looked up from the needlepoint version of Harley Quinn's baseball bat she was doing for a customer who was really into cosplay. It was going onto a satin jacket and the work was super detailed.

The girls stood at the counter. They went to Suttonville… probably…but Lucy didn't know them. The petite girl holding the purple corset with the bats had an almost matching purple streak in her hair.

"Oh," Lucy said, appreciative. "That's perfect for you."

The tiny girl stood taller and her friend — a slim, blond cheerleader type — rolled her eyes. "Don't encourage her."

"Why not?" Lucy beamed at the tiny girl. "Something tells me you enjoy a little mayhem, yes?"

The tiny girl's eyes widened. "Why yes, I do."

Lucy nodded. "Thought so. Pair that corset with a black tutu and ripped tights, and you'll slay Halloween."

"I'll take it." The girl handed her a credit card.

"You didn't ask how much." Lucy frowned. The corset was a hundred and twenty-five dollars.

The tiny girl waved a hand. "No price is too much for a slayed Halloween. I'm having a party, and I want everything to be epic." She pointed at her friend. "Epic, I say."

I do *like customers with money. Customers with sass* and *money are even better.* "Your wish is my command. I always have unique pieces, in case you need something else. I'm Lucy. Just ask for me when you come in."

The tiny girl nodded toward her friend. "How about something for her?"

The cheerleader girl shot her friend an affectionate, if annoyed, glance. "Speaking of tutus, how much is the pink one, with the ballet shoes on it."

"Eighty."

"My little sis will love it." She forked over a credit card, too. Lucy grinned. Mom would freak when she heard that Lucy had sold two pieces before noon. She did a steady trade, especially through an online specialty shop, but selling two big pieces at the store was unheard of. She charged the girls' cards, then wrapped their buys. "You two come back sometime."

"You have talent," the cheerleader said in admiration. "I've never seen embroidery like this before. Where did you learn to do it?"

"My grandma was big into needlepoint. She taught me when I was little, mostly to keep me busy and out of trouble. I added my own spin later." Lucy shrugged, hiding the pride fluttering in her chest. "It's a fun hobby."

The tiny girl shook her head. "Not hobby. Art."

"Thanks, I appreciate that." Lucy waved as they left the shop, then danced around behind the counter for a full minute. It had taken a year to convince her mom to show some of her pieces in the store. *"It's for older ladies who like to quilt, hon. Your work is…a little too avant-garde for my regulars."* Now, though, people who never would've come by stopped in to look at the crazy needlepoint designs. Most of them even bought something.

Lucy went to the workroom in the back of the shop and settled into her chair. The bright lamp she used when doing detail work shown hot onto the satin jacket as she picked up her needle and continued to stitch the "d" in "Good Night." The diamond patterns had turned out great, and if she could finish the lettering by today, she could move onto the clockwork storks on the baby blanket commission she'd received yesterday, along with the other three projects still waiting.

This was going to be a busy summer.

The bell above the front door *dinged*, and her mom's voice floated back to the workroom. "I know it starts Monday. I didn't forget. It's just that I have that quilting seminar starting. Let's ask Lucy. I'm sure she can drive you."

"But she always gets lost!" Otis protested. *"Always.* She got lost taking me home from school, and she *went there!"*

"Hey!" Lucy called. "I haven't been at Bluebonnet for six years. Cut me some slack."

Her nine-year-old brother stepped into the doorway, scowling. "It's two blocks from home."

"I missed *one turn*, doofus." Lucy laughed. "But what are y'all talking about?"

Mom stopped by Lucy's worktable, nodding appreciatively at the jacket. "That's turning out nice. Not sure why a grown woman wants a cartoon baseball bat on a two-hundred-dollar jacket, but you've done well with it."

Lucy flushed. Mom's praise was a rare thing—it had to be earned. "Thanks. But where am I taking Otis?"

"Oh! He starts that half-day baseball camp at the high school on Monday. I have a new quilting class at the exact same time for the next two weeks, so I need you to drive him."

Otis let his forehead fall against the wall. "We'll get loosssst."

Lucy rolled her eyes. "I know where Suttonville High is. I've gone there for three years, remember? We won't get lost."

"Of course you won't," Mom said, trying not to laugh. "And Lucy has GPS on her phone if you're that worried."

"Doesn't matter." Otis sounded so despondent that Lucy laughed.

"You are one dramatic nine-year-old." She went back to stitching the jacket. She could totally drive to school, and the athletic fields had to be behind the main campus somewhere. "It'll be fine. I promise."

"Okay." He clomped by on his way to the tiny room Mom had set up as a playroom when Lucy was little and she'd had to bring her to work. When Otis inherited it, he'd taken out the dolls and installed a PlayStation. "We have to be there at eight-thirty to register, and the camp starts at nine. The Sentinels won state, and their best pitcher will be my coach, so we can't be late."

"I swear I'll have you there by eight-thirty." Because why wouldn't she be up at such an ungodly hour on a Monday during summer? And who would want to spend three hours hitting balls with sticks? Still, she'd do anything for Otis. He'd wrapped her around his little finger the first time she'd laid eyes on the chubby newborn at the hospital. And he knew it. "Mom, Serena and I want to go out tomorrow night."

"Where are you going? When will you be home?"

"Why always two questions at once? Why so suspicious?"

Lucy grinned at her mother's pursed mouth. "Okay, okay. We're going to the lake. Serena's dad is letting us take the boat out for a few hours."

Mom's eyes narrowed. "Is that all?"

Lucy held up her hands. "What else could there be?"

"I still remember receiving a call saying you and Serena stole a dog from down the street."

Lucy scowled. "The owner was abusing the poor thing."

"And what about the time you spray painted 'Down with Fascists' on a placard outside city hall?"

At least she hadn't sprayed it on the wall…and she'd done four hours of community service for it, too. "They're voting to stop allowing livestock inside town lines. Serena's dad is worried they won't let him keep his free-range farm!"

Mom crossed her arms. "And the time you were out until one chasing shooting stars?"

Lucy squirmed. "That was two years ago."

"Honey, I have no problem with you hanging out with Serena. Just…try to temper the passion a little, huh?" She patted Lucy's back and went to the front to work on receipts.

Lucy flopped into her chair. Curb her passions? It wasn't enough that she was working her butt off on her needlepoint, but she'd been helping in the store and watching Otis, too. With Dad stationed overseas, she'd really reined it in to help her mom, but a girl needed a little mischief from time to time. She wasn't hurting anyone, and she never would. All her "incidents" came from a helpful place. So what if she was kind of a mess—life was messy, and she fully intended to live it.

Chapter Three

Dylan was in the dugout, preparing the equipment, by seven-thirty Monday morning. When Tristan stumbled in at eight, looking like he needed a giant cup of coffee, he groaned. "Dylan, man, this is excessive. They're little leaguers."

"It's recruiting." He threw a couple more balls into the pitchers' box. "We're teachers. We need to be on top of stuff."

Tristan grumbled but came to help drag everything out onto the field. Water jugs were set up on tables outside the foul lines on third and first, the grass was freshly mowed, and the infield dirt was pristine. If that didn't impress the parents who shelled out three hundred bucks for this camp, Dylan didn't know what would. This would be the best camp the Sentinels ever put on—that was the mission.

The first campers started showing up for registration around eight-twenty. A few underclassmen were working the sign-in table, sending kids to Dylan if they were pitchers, and to Tristan if they were outfielders. Nate Rodriquez had the infielders. He was an upcoming junior and a wicked shortstop. They made a good set of captains.

The first kid through the gate ran straight at Tristan. "I'm Corey and you're Tristan Murrell."

"Hi, Corey." He shot Dylan an amused look over Corey's head. "You play centerfield?"

"Just like you!" The kid prattled on as Tristan directed him farther out into the field.

Nate watched, laughing. "Remember being that age and thinking the high school guys were heroes?"

Dylan nodded. "That's why I want this to be perfect. These kids don't know we're human."

"Aw, c'mon. We *are* human. I'm a Mexican-Irish kid who hates tamales *and* shepherd's pie. If that's not human, I don't know what is."

"I'd eat both of those things." Dylan watched as more cars rolled up and kids climbed out. "I don't mean act untouchable… I meant we have to preserve the illusion. It's like at Disney World—you have to be at least sixteen to do the 'Behind the Magic' tour. They want to save the magic for the kids. They look up to us, you know?"

"Hey!" Jeremy Ledecky, their new right fielder, came jogging over. "Two campers forgot their gloves. Think Coach will care if I pull some from the equipment room?"

"That's fine. I'll take over your check-in table."

Dylan went to Ledecky's seat and picked up a pen. If kids were pitchers, he introduced himself and sent them to stand on the pitcher's mound. Almost all his little pitchers were here, except one: Otis Foster. Dylan checked his phone… eight fifty-nine. Camp was about to start. He couldn't wait to see if Otis would show up. They'd have to start without him.

Sighing, he collected the sign-in sheets, grabbed his glove, and headed to the mound. "Good morning, guys!"

"Good morning, Coach!" they shouted.

Coach…that had a nice ring to it. After the majors, he wanted to coach college ball. This would be good training. He smiled at the wiggling, bouncing campers. "Okay, first things first, we always warm up. Put your gloves down and do what I do."

Dylan stretched his arms up to the sky, checking over his shoulder to make sure the boys were following suit. They were. Good. He lowered his arms and stretched them out to his sides, then twisted slowly at the waist. He had them touch their toes, stretch their triceps, and roll their shoulders.

"Okay, let's go for a little jog. Down the foul line just past first, then turn behind second and come up the third base foul line. Ready? Go!"

The boys took off more at a sprint that a jog, and Dylan chuckled. He jogged behind them, keeping an eye on the kids lagging behind. Before the end of camp, he'd push those guys a little to bring them up to pace.

"Excuse me!" a girl waved at him from behind the first base side fence. Through the chain link, he could see a boy standing next to her looking miserable.

The girl was about his age, and dressed in ripped jeans, a T-shirt that read "Free Range" in hot pink, and Converse with flowers painted in glitter on them. Her ponytail hung over one shoulder, the tips as pink as the letters on her shirt. She looked like she belonged in an incense shop, not at a ballpark. She was pretty, though, in a flower-child kind of way.

"Yes?" he asked politely, standing up straighter and hoping she'd take a look. Pure reflex reaction to a pretty girl, even if girls were on the no-fly list.

The boy at her side squirmed. "I'm Otis, and I'm late because my sister got lost." He shot her a look that would be angry if it weren't kind of cute. "Again."

"I said I was sorry. Besides, you're only…" She looked at a yellow plastic watch on her right arm. "Ten minutes late."

"I'm fourteen minutes late," Otis grumbled.

"It's okay, Otis," Dylan said. "The other guys are warming up. Let me take your bag while you jog around the bases and meet them, huh?"

Otis gave him a relieved smile and took off. He was fast—probably the fastest kid on the field. His cleats were a little worn, but his workout clothes fit him well. This kid took playing ball seriously. Dylan could appreciate that.

"So, um," the girl was saying. "What time do you finish?"

Dylan stared at her. "Noon. We finish at noon."

She frowned at him. "No need to be snippy."

Snippy? He frowned. That wasn't at all what—

"Lucy!" Otis jogged over from the mound. "Leave Coach alone."

"Coach?" The girl—Lucy—looked him up and down. "He's my age, tops."

"And what age would that be?" Dylan asked, trying not to be offended. What was this girl's problem?

"An incoming senior." She stared him down, and he was startled by her eyes. They were the oddest shade of brown he'd ever seen—light, with more gold than chocolate. When she turned more into the sun, they looked greenish. Hazel?

He gaped at her, unable to stop looking at those amazing eyes. She had him completely off balance, but he kind of liked it.

And then he realized what she'd said.

"Wait, you go to school here?" he asked. "And you got lost?"

Lucy's mouth set in a hard line. "I've never been to the ball fields. In my defense, this isn't the main part of campus, you know. I tried to take a shortcut. Turns out it was a dead end."

Okay, that was funny. Dylan bit back a smile. "So…um, I'll send Otis out to you when camp's over?"

She crossed her arms. Her long, brown hair blew in the wind, the pink tips fluttering. "I think I'll stick around, make sure he's okay. I brought things to work on."

What, does she think we can't manage a handful of nine-year-olds? "He'll be fine. We even have a nurse on staff. Anything happens, we'll call you right away."

There, that sounded professional, right?

But Lucy frowned, and he could tell she was digging in. "I'm staying."

Dylan barely kept from rolling his eyes. This girl was nice to look at, but he couldn't stand here and argue with her all morning. "Suit yourself. The bleachers are open."

She nodded. Dylan watched her over his shoulder as he walked to the mound to set up for practice. Lucy marched to her car and retrieved a large canvas bag, then went to the bleachers, where some moms were watching practice. She didn't choose the shade, though. Instead, she put on a pair of lightly tinted sunglasses and sat out in the full sun.

"What's she doing?" Dylan asked, when her brother came back from his jog.

Otis sighed. "Sewing."

"For real?"

"For real. I guess she decided to stay, Coach. My sister is pretty cool, but when she gets something into her head, she's not gonna move."

Dylan heard the affection—and exasperation—in Otis's high-pitched voice. Obviously, she was decent sister...but potentially a walking train wreck at the same time. "Okay, then. Let's get to work."

He called all the young pitchers over, along with their freshman catcher, and began his assessment.

Chapter Four

Of all the infuriating, stuffy, stick-up-the-ass ball players. Lucy fumed as she searched for a seat with good light that wouldn't burn her retinas at the same time. So what if she got lost? The ball fields were at the very end of school property, in a field that wasn't even remotely attached to the main parking lot. She'd had to circle twice to figure out where the sports complex lot was. It was an honest mistake, really.

And that Coach guy looked like he might be as fun as a root canal without laughing gas. Too bad, because he was cute as hell. Blond, blue-eyed, tallish, great shoulders, nice butt. She'd taken a good hard look as he led the little pitchers through their first drill. Still, Coach struck her as the kind of guy who only read baseball books and took everything *way* too seriously. Definitely not her type.

Lucy bent over her baby blanket. It was sweaty work, hand-embroidering a wool blanket in the Texas-in-July sun, even if it was only nine-thirty. But she had to finish it, and she didn't have time to waste these days. She didn't feel good about leaving Otis by himself, though. Part of it was her over-protective streak, but part of it was pride, and she knew that. She was scared if she left, she'd lose track of time and show up late to pick up Otis. Not for the first time, she cursed her inability to maintain her sense of time or direction. Mom said it was because she was so right-brained and creative, but Lucy wondered if there was something wrong with her internal compass *and* her internal clock.

As she sweated and stitched, *tings* from metal bats and the *whomp* of balls in gloves filtered up from the field. Little boys chattered, followed by the deeper voices of their coaches.

Coaches. She snorted. More like high school guys living out their hero worship.

Except...

"Otis!" His coach's voice rang out. "That was fantastic!"

Lucy's head snapped up to see Otis dance around on the pitcher's mound. His coach patted him on the shoulder, then squatted so he was eye level with her brother, pointing and gesturing. Otis soaked in every word, standing more still than she'd ever seen. Finally, he nodded at his coach, put the ball in his glove, then wound up and pitched. The high school guy at the plate caught it, then mimed shaking his hand out, like Otis's pitch had been hard enough to hurt.

His coach laughed and gave Otis a fist bump before calling up the next kid. Her brother was beaming with pride. Ever since Dad had been called up from the reserves to active duty in February, Otis had barely smiled, but today he stood tall. A pang of envy ate at Lucy's stomach. She'd tried so hard to keep him happy while Dad was overseas, but a guy Otis barely knew could make him grin where she couldn't.

Tears stung her eyes. Dad had been gone five months and might be gone five more before they saw him again. He understood her better than Mom did. So it wasn't just Otis who had trouble smiling these days.

After an hour, the sun beat down on her too much, and Lucy was forced into the shade. Determined to work, she used the flashlight on her phone to illuminate the tiny gear joints on a stork's leg. She'd decided to put a caterpillar with a top hat on the corner as a little extra touch, but she didn't have the thread for it, so she worked to finish the stork so she could really detail the caterpillar back at her worktable.

"Look at that," a woman said. "What gorgeous work."

Lucy looked up and smiled. "Melody's Quilt Shop. We do custom pieces, and we have some ready made."

"Is that the cute little place in historic downtown?" the woman next to her asked. She nudged her friend. "The tea room is two doors down. We should do some shopping."

"Definitely." The women gave her friendly nods before turning back to watch the boys play.

Well, if nothing else, sweating her butt off was resulting in potential sales. Serena found it hilarious that Lucy would worry about this stuff when she was only seventeen, but after she graduated high school and studied business and apparel design in college, Lucy had plans to open her own sewing shop. Maybe even build up a chain. All with a needle, a few specialty embroidery machines, and lots of thread. Sure, she had more orders than she could handle at the moment, but if it got her name out there, she'd forego some sleep.

Practice ended precisely at noon, Otis's coach calling the others in. He must be more than just the pitching coach— He was the ringleader. There was an older man watching everything, probably the high school coach, but his team was running the show.

Lucy took her time packing up her supplies, waiting for the field to clear. Otis stuck to his coach like a burr on a wool sock, following him around, helping clean up all the gear. When Lucy made it to the gate, Otis pretended not to notice.

The coach shot her a wry smile and guided her brother over.

"You did great today. Go home, rest that arm—a little ice is good. We'll work on hitting tomorrow."

"Thanks, Coach Dylan! See you tomorrow!" Otis came through the gate, waving, his bag slung over his shoulder. "That was awesome, Lu. I want to be early tomorrow, okay?"

"Sure." She glanced back at the coach. "Is his last name or first name Dylan?"

"First name. He wouldn't let me call him Coach Dennings." Otis laughed. "He said that sounded too much like his dad."

Dylan Dennings. Lucy didn't think she'd heard his name before, but Suttonville was a huge school, and she knew barely a third of the students in her class. Plus, she didn't run with the athletic, popular, or rich crowd. Her friends tended to be more interesting.

"Glad you had fun, Squirt. Let's grab some lunch and head to the shop."

"Burgers?" Otis asked, eyes pleading.

At least he didn't suggest chicken nuggets, which was all he ate for the first two months Dad was gone. "Burgers it is. In fact, I'll take you to Dolly's for a shake to go with it."

Otis whooped and raced for the car. Lucy paused, sensing eyes on her back. When she turned, she found Dylan watching her.

She couldn't decide if she liked it or not.

"Dylan Dennings," Serena said, forehead scrunched up. "Blond?"

"Yeah. He's cute but way too...stiff for my taste."

"Hey." Serena waggled her eyebrows, jangling the eyebrow ring above her right eye. "'Stiff' is a trait I want in a certain part of a guy."

"Oh my God." Lucy covered her face. "I was *not* talking about that. He's…serious. The look he gave me when we showed up late? It was like I personally disappointed him. It's *just* baseball camp, not a congressional hearing, or something."

"Hmm. But he's cute?"

Lucy nodded. "And he was nice to Otis."

"Total fixer-upper." Serena grinned. "If I wasn't smitten, I'd give a guy like that a shot."

"And how is the love of your life these days?"

"Cuddly as a teddy bear and as skilled as a romance novel hero." Serena winked. "I think he's still kind of surprised I asked him out, but we get along pretty well."

Lucy wasn't sure she wanted to imagine Serena's boyfriend in the sack—no, she was *absolutely* sure she didn't—but her friend hadn't been this feisty in a while, so she let it pass. "Good. What about when he leaves for school?"

Serena shrugged and handed Lucy a shovel. "We'll play it by ear. SMU is only forty minutes away. It's not like he's going out of state."

Lucy wished she could be so matter-of-fact about guys. "I guess that's better than being single and bored with high school guys."

"You haven't found the right one, yet. They aren't all immature assholes." Serena led Lucy out into the pasture, where they were greeted by joyous clucking. "Seriously, I think you ought to check out this Dylan guy."

"I don't date athletes. I like guys who, you know, *read* instead of watch ESPN all night long." Lucy sighed. "I think I'll say forget it until I'm in college. I want a guy with fire for something more than a kegger by the lake. Someone willing to go ziplining in Peru, backpacking in Australia, or museum hopping in Paris. Someone *fun*, multi-dimensional."

"Mine's taken." Serena flashed her a smile. "Cheer up. Maybe the boyfriend fairy will drop Mr. Perfect in your lap.

Now, let's get busy. These hens need to go to bed so we can go out."

Lucy filled a tin cup full of freeze-dried mealworms and shook it as Serena called, "Here, chickies. Here chick, chick, chick!"

Forty hens scurried in their direction. In the chicken run on the other side of the fence, a protest of clucking started when the hens realized they had to wait for their turn. Lucy laughed and left a trail of worms for the chickens to lure them into the coop. Serena's dad had four large chicken runs across the two acres behind their farmhouse. They were technically inside town limits, but barely. That's what made Lucy so mad about the pending ordinance. Their nearest neighbor was six acres away— The chickens weren't bothering anyone, and they ate all the grubs and slugs off the tomato beds, not to mention the mosquitos. Plus, their dog, Millie, was awesome at chasing off hawks and herding the hens if they were too rowdy. It was the perfect operation.

After settling the last flock into their coop, Serena and Lucy went into the work shed to pull off their rubber boots and change into sandals. A soft breeze rustled the feedbags by the door, and Lucy breathed deep. Most people wouldn't enjoy a chicken farm, but she did. The chickens were funny and cute, and her mom appreciated fresh eggs. Lucy would've helped around the farm for free, but she usually walked out with a dozen organic, free-range eggs.

She followed Serena around the side of the house to the car. Her dad had left behind his beloved Jeep Wrangler, allowing Lucy to drive it until he was back home. "North pier, right?

"Yep. I brought some cookies and stuff. It's a nice night for a little cruise." Serena hopped into the passenger seat. "And if we happen to pull up a few campaign signs for the mayor on the way, so be it."

Lucy gave her a tight smile. "So be it."

Chapter Five

DYLAN

Dylan pulled himself, dripping, into the back of Tristan's dad's ski boat. "I'm rusty."

Tristan snorted and took the rope from him. He'd already put the ski back in its rack. "You stayed up for three minutes. If we hadn't hit that wake, you wouldn't have fallen at all. Stop being so hard on yourself."

"You know me," Dylan said. "I don't like falling."

"Yeah, I know you all right." Tristan restarted the boat, cruising toward the pier. "We need gas, and it's getting dark. Let's grab some drinks and just drive a while."

"Fine by me." Dylan stretched out on the seat in the bow of the ski boat. "I told Mom I wouldn't be back for dinner, so I'm up for whatever."

"I think this is the first night it's just been the two of us in a while." Tristan guided the boat up to the gas pump at the side of the dock. "I'm glad Swing Away's so busy, but it sucks that Alyssa always has to work late."

"They deserve the business," Dylan said, hoping he didn't sound lonely or desperate.

Tristan nudged Dylan's foot as he took a seat. "What about you? We need to find you a girl."

"Nope." Dylan shook his head. "No girls until I make it."

"Dude, you aren't some kind of monk." Tristan tossed him a soda can, cold and dripping with condensation. "It's senior year. You want to go to prom, right?"

That girl—Lucy—popped up in Dylan's mind. *Yeah, no.* She struck him as hard to please. She'd probably complain about his dancing.

Dylan snorted, and Tristan cocked his head. "What, do you already have a date planned?"

"I'll take a friend or something." Dylan turned to stare at the water. Tristan's gaze felt like pity, even if he didn't mean it to be. "Maybe Lauren, if ten guys don't ask her first."

"Better you than me," Tristan muttered.

When Dylan had been trying to catch Alyssa's attention, her best friend Lauren slipped into his life. They were friends. That's it. They texted and hit the occasional movie—she liked Marvel movies, and her friends didn't—but nothing more.

"You aren't still mad at me for trying to help set you up with her, are you?" Dylan chuckled. "Because that was pretty funny."

"It's funny *now,*" Tristan said. "Not eight weeks ago."

He started up the boat, and they cruised out onto the lake, which was crowded with people enjoying the sunset. Another ski-boat, this one filled with girls, floated by, all of them whistling and giggling as they passed. Dylan flushed and draped a towel over his shoulders.

"I can't go anywhere after that homerun derby, asshat," he said to Tristan. "There are pictures of my chest on the internet."

"Mine, too," Tristan chuckled. "But the homerun derby

is why my girlfriend has to work late every night this week. Small price to pay for her happiness, I guess."

They continued around the lake, nice and slow, enjoying the breeze. The water was calm, with only a few ripples and some chop from boat wakes. Dylan felt himself relax for the first time in months.

That's when the calls for help started.

Tristan's head whipped around, and he turned the boat almost immediately after. From the sound of things, the cries were coming from two girls toward the middle of the lake. Dylan stood, searching for whoever was out there.

"I see it." He pointed to a shadowy blob that turned out to be a small motorboat. Two girls were flagging them down. "Come in closer and I'll tie us together."

Tristan guided their boat alongside the girls' boat, keeping a safe distance between them, and Dylan tossed a rope across. "Tie in!"

"Thank you so much!" A tall, well-built girl with red-blond hair called. "Our gas gauge must be broken. It's reading half a tank, but we ran out."

Dylan helped Tristan pull the boat closer to theirs but almost let go of the rope when he caught sight of the other girl. "Lucy?"

Lucy peered at him and groaned. "Coach Dylan? God, just my luck."

Dylan couldn't have retorted even if he'd had something to say ready on his tongue. Lucy was wearing a bright blue bikini top with a flowing cotton skirt over the bottoms. The T-shirt and jeans had hidden one hell of a figure, and smooth, fair skin. His jaw worked, nothing coming out.

"Coach Dylan?" Tristan gave him an amused look. "I'm pretty sure you can call him just Dylan."

"Okay, Just Dylan." Lucy put a hand on her hip. "I suppose this calamity is another black mark on my record, huh?"

"No," Tristan said quickly. "It could happen to anyone. Aren't you the sister of that good little pitcher today?"

"Otis? Yes."

The other girl draped herself over the boat bench, batting her eyelashes. "And I'm her best friend, Serena. You boys doing anything after towing us in?"

"Tristan has a girlfriend," Dylan said. Better for him to look rude— Lucy already thought he was an asshole. "And I'm at his mercy. It's a long swim back."

Serena laughed. "You're so cute, but I was just messing with you. I'm taken. Lucy's single, though. In case you need a swim partner."

Tristan made a choking noise, and Dylan shot him a dirty look. "Uh, about that. I'm not on the market."

"Girlfriend?" Serena asked, head cocked like she was all ears.

"Um, no. Just…other stuff."

"Wait one damn minute." Lucy crossed her arms. "For real, or is it me?"

"Okay, that's not fair." Dylan spread his hands, wondering how the hell he'd walked into that one. "I don't even know you."

"It's me." She glowered at him. "Don't bother trying so hard."

"Oh, be honest, you wouldn't go out with me in a million years, either," Dylan shot back. "Oil and water."

Serena's smile grew shrewd. "Prove it."

Lucy turned her glare on Serena. "Stop. Now."

"Why? You're right— He is cute."

Dylan's face burned red hot. "Wait…you told someone I'm cute? You were talking about me?"

Lucy didn't answer. Instead she stalked to the front of their boat and sat with her back turned.

"Nice move, jackass," Tristan whispered, then louder,

"Serena, we can't tow you back—that's dangerous, but we'll go for gas, if you want."

"Let me swim over. I have money." She looked back at Lucy, and Dylan could tell something crazy was about to happen. "I don't want Lucy left alone out here. Send Dylan over. He can hang with her until we're back."

"Or I could go, and you could stay with him." Lucy's tone was half mortified, half sour.

"I wouldn't dream of it." And before Lucy could protest further, Serena had tightened her life vest and jumped into the water.

Tristan stepped up close to Dylan. "You owe Lucy an apology. We'll only be gone ten minutes. I think it's a good idea you stay here."

He was right, but that didn't make Dylan like it any better. "Okay, okay."

Not sure how any of this had happened, Dylan jumped off the ski deck and started swimming for Serena's boat.

Chapter Six

Lucy watched Dylan cut through the water with a precise breaststroke. Even his swimming was neat and tidy. She slumped against the bench as he pulled himself onboard and untied the boys' boat. He stood there, dripping, while their friends cruised away.

"Um…" He swallowed hard and wiped water out of his eyes. "Look—"

"Don't bother." She slumped as far as she could without falling off the bench. "I know what you meant. Just because our friends set us up doesn't mean we have to do anything about it."

"Hey." He sounded irritated now. "You don't understand, and that's why I'm here. I'm not dating because I'm focused entirely on baseball right now. I have a shot at the minors next spring after we graduate, and I'm putting all my energy into that. It's not you." He rubbed his face, shifting his balance like he was going to jump out of the boat any second. "You're…

you're...well, you're someone I would definitely chat up under different circumstances."

Lucy slowly sat up straighter, noticing how his ears had turned red. The little devil on her shoulder, the one that made her impulsive, talked her into pulling her shoulders back and pushing her chest out ever so slightly. Just to see what he'd do. When his eyes drifted, then snapped back to her face, she smirked a little. "Chat me up, huh? Even though you think I'm a hot mess?"

"Did I ever say that?" He crossed his arms over his life vest. "Maybe I questioned your ability to drive places, but I never said you were a mess."

"Uh huh." She relaxed against the seat, unable to believe it. "You seemed really annoyed that I stayed for camp today. I could almost see the thought bubble over your head, 'this one's brought his crazy sister.'"

"I didn't..." He squeezed his eyes shut and ground his jaw. After a deep breath, he tried again. "I just thought you were a little overprotective. Otis is nine, not two."

"And who are you to decide that?" Lucy sat up straighter, daring him to look her over. "But, if you want, I'll stay away from your precious camp. You better take good care of my brother, though, or we'll have more than words, *Coach Dylan*."

She sighed, furious that she'd taken the bait and engaged with this jackass. "You don't have to stand there like you're about to jump in the lake if I twitch in your direction. I wouldn't touch you if you paid me."

Dylan's eyes narrowed. As if he was calling her bluff, he unbuckled his life vest and dropped it to the floor. *Oh, shirtless boy alert.*

Yep, she was right...he *was* cute. And cut. His blond hair was tinged gold by the setting sun, but her gaze kept straying somewhere else...somewhere tan and muscular. As she watched, his forearms tensed, showing off a pair of arms that demanded her attention.

She met his eyes and found him smirking back at her. Right. "I appreciate the effort, but you're not my type."

He rolled his eyes. "You're not exactly mine, either, Princess."

She rose, standing with her feet wide apart to compensate for the rocking boat. "And what type is that? Bubble headed? Simpering? Compliant?"

He glared at her. "Disciplined. Smart. Driven."

She laughed coldly. "I think that's the wrong kind of girl for you. Too much like-knows-like. You need someone to shake you up, make you live for now instead of a year from now."

"Oh, and you think you're the person to do that?"

For some reason, both their voices had risen, but she couldn't back down. Mom would tell her the passion was getting the better of her, and if only she took a second to breathe, she'd see it. Too late for that now. "I might be, if you removed the stick from your ass."

He took a step toward her. "Yeah, and *you* need someone to untangle your hot-mess self."

She took a big step toward him, pointing a finger at his chest. "I knew you thought I was a hot mess!"

He took another step, but she wasn't afraid of him. No, she didn't think she'd ever felt so alive, honestly. Her heart pounded in her chest, and her fingertips tingled. Like she'd been in a dim room, and someone had turned on a floodlight.

"Fine! I *did* think it, and I'll say it, too," Dylan snapped. "You're a hot mess, Lucy Foster. What are you going to do about it?"

Her mouth dropped open, and her whole body flushed with heat. The next step she took brought her an inch away from him. Close enough to see he was shaking. Rage? Fear? All she knew was that she was shaking, too, but it was from neither of those things. "You know what I think? I think you're a jackass!"

Then, before she could decide whether this was the worst idea she'd ever had, she swayed closer, so that her chest brushed his just *barely*, and went up on tiptoe, stopping short of kissing him…waiting to see what would happen.

They stared each other down, each of them breathing hard. Lucy's gaze dropped to his lips then back to his eyes, daring him to make a move.

He growled, this frustrated, almost anguished sound, before closing the distance. He pulled her close, his wet torso sliding slick against hers. Then his mouth was on hers, and she forgot everything—about being angry, about being stuck in the middle of the lake with a guy who pushed her buttons, about Dad being gone. Nothing mattered but his warm breath against her cheek and his strong arms holding her tight despite the rocking boat beneath them. Good thing, because she was lightheaded, but didn't want to come up for air.

They clung together, the kiss frantic and disorganized. Somewhere in the back of her brain, she recognized this guy hadn't let himself go for a long, long time…and that he'd been hurt recently. All of it was there in the depth of this kiss. His chest was warm, heaving against hers, and his fingers traced the line of her bare spine, sending shivers across her back.

She didn't even hear the other boat approach. No, she didn't notice a thing until Serena called, "Sweet baby Jesus! I said apologize, not act out a movie star kiss in the middle of my boat!"

Dylan broke away from her, looking startled and a little ashamed. "Sorry. I don't know why… I better go."

He jumped into the lake before she could answer. Lucy stood there, dumbfounded, before noticing he'd left his vest in the boat. "Hey, you forgot something."

She tossed it in his general direction. To her surprise, he

caught it easily, and shrugged it on in the water, as Serena threw a rope across to bring the boats closer so she could clamber over with a gas can. Dylan didn't even look at her as Tristan waited to make sure their boat would start. Once it did, Lucy murmured, "Get me out of here."

Serena nodded and gunned the engine, waving and calling out thanks as they pulled away. Once they were almost to the pier, she slowed the boat. "What the unholy hell was that?"

"I have no idea." Tears welled in Lucy's eyes. "I really don't. We were yelling—I mean *really* yelling—at each other. Then, all of a sudden, I'm an inch away, and we're kissing. It was the craziest thing ever." She pressed a hand to her mouth. "God, I'm so embarrassed."

Serena gaped at her. "*Why?* That looked like the kind of kiss to bring a girl to her knees."

Lucy let out a half-sob half-giggle. "Yeah, it was. Thing is, I still don't know if he thinks I'm an idiot or not."

"He doesn't. In fact, I'm pretty sure *he* feels like the idiot for bolting the way he did." Serena shrugged. "You'll see him tomorrow, right? Push his buttons a bit, see what happens."

That wasn't a bad idea. Except, Lucy had no idea how she felt about him. Was the kiss something about hate and lust crossing a line somewhere, or was she actually interested? Cute was one thing. Starting something with a type A, ultra-disciplined athlete was the last possible thing she'd ever consider. Plus, she had way too much going on to give *that* a try. Still…he had this vibe, this sense of pain and of wanting something more, underneath that shell. Thinking about him tugged at her in a strange way, wondering about this too-together, sort of brokenish guy. She didn't know who'd hurt him, but it was there, gasping for air. He needed to have his heart knit back together, whether he believed it or not.

And she knew someone who was damn good with a needle.

Chapter Seven

DYLAN

Dylan let his head hang in his hands. "What did I do? What did I *do*?"

Tristan laughed. "You kissed a gorgeous girl in the middle of the lake at sunset. Why are you acting like you killed a bunny?"

"Because we were fighting...I think. Then we were kissing. Shit, I don't know." It was kind of a blur, actually, but he remembered yelling something stupid. He couldn't remember why, though. Then Lucy was pressed up against him and his brain misfired, and...Dylan groaned. "What's wrong with me?"

"Nothing." Tristan punched him lightly in the shoulder. "Opposites attract sometimes."

"No one is as opposite as I am with this girl." Dylan sat up, feeling like his nerves had short-circuited. "I met her *today*. I've never, ever in my life kissed a girl I barely know. Not once. There are steps you take first. You get her number.

You hang out some. *Then*, you kiss her."

"Dude, really? There are times I think you were born a hundred years too late," Tristan said. "Hell, Alyssa kissed me the day after I met her. It was to make me swing without thinking, but still."

Like he needed that reminder. "Not helping."

"Sorry, man."

The cautious tone hurt Dylan worse. He knew Tristan still felt guilty for ending up with Alyssa when Dylan liked her first, and yeah, it stung, but he wasn't mad at anyone. Tristan and Alyssa were good together. He wasn't going to pout over that. And how could he? He'd just planted one on a delicious brunette—he had no room to be upset with anyone.

Dylan sighed. "Okay, whatever. Tomorrow, I'm going to act like nothing happened."

"No!" Tristan said. "You have to discuss the elephant."

"But how?" Dylan looked at his friend. "I'm sure she wants to forget it happened, too."

"Do you really want to forget?" Tristan asked, his look shrewd. "Or are you freaked out because it caught you off guard? We all know how much you hate to move outside the pattern. You have a goal, and you march toward it. That's what's wrong—you're not upset you kissed her. You're upset it didn't go according to plan."

"That's not true." But it was, at least a little bit. What had Lucy said? Something about living for now instead of a year from now? The thought scared the hell out of him.

And it excited him, too. If he was completely honest with himself, a little chaos sounded…fun. But chaos led to missed opportunities. He'd have to take this slow.

Tristan was watching him, so Dylan nodded. "Okay. I'll talk to her tomorrow, see where we are."

"Good." Tristan pushed the boat's motor up to full speed. "Let's go home so we can rest up. I swear, those campers wore me out today."

Dylan pretended to joke along as they drove back, but the look on Lucy's face when he dove off the boat was the only thing on his mind.

He needed to fix this.

When Dylan came home, his mom took one look at him and pointed wordlessly at the tray of cookies cooling on the stove. How she knew exactly what he needed just by looking at his face, he hadn't figured out. Mom radar. "Do I look like I need a cookie?"

"You look like you need a dozen." She smiled fondly. "But you won't eat more than two."

"Sugar in, garbage out." The cookies were really good, though. "Where's Dad?"

"Dinner in the city. New clients, I think." Mom stretched and stood. "I'm headed to bed now that you're home safe."

"Night."

Mom waved and headed for her room, their cats— *her* cats—following behind. Those little bastards ignored everyone else now that his sister was in France on a college exchange program. Without Tori home, the house was always quiet on nights when Dad was out on business. No game on in the living room, no midnight calls to India. His dad's presence left a hole when he wasn't around.

Dylan wandered upstairs to his room, not sure what he wanted to do. He didn't want to think, but a silent house wasn't distracting enough to make his brain stop. He went through his bedtime routine silently, mulling over what Tristan said. Was he really that inflexible? He didn't feel like he was. If you wanted something badly enough, you had to have discipline in everything, or anything could knock you off balance. Like kissing a girl on a boat after a shouting match.

He sank into bed and plugged in his phone. Maybe Lucy wouldn't even drive Otis to camp. Maybe she'd check Otis in while Dylan was busy.

Or maybe she'd show up angry, demanding an explanation.

Dylan wished he was callous enough not to care. There were guys on his team who went through girls like two-ply. Not guys he liked to hang with, though. Sure, he'd gone out with four girls in the last three years, but he hadn't been an asshole about ending a relationship. He liked girls, a lot, and some of his older sister's boyfriends had taught him how *not* to treat a girl.

Maybe that's why he kept rejecting the idea of a quick summer fling with a wild girl. God, he was so boring. Lucy wasn't even all that wild...so far as he could tell, anyway.

Tired, and knowing sleep was even more important than diet when it came to performance, he rolled over and pulled the comforter up to his ears. He'd worry about all this crap in the morning.

Clouds hung on the western horizon and the wind blew dust up from the infield as Dylan and Nate checked in their campers. Nate kept looking up at the sky, brow furrowed. "I don't know, man. We might make it until noon, we might not."

"We can always take them into the team room and watch film." Dylan checked in another outfielder and sent him running out to Tristan. "But this stuff is supposed to hold off until two."

Nate glanced at the clouds. "If you say so. My *abuela* brought all her plants onto the back porch this morning. I trust her more than a weather app."

"I would, too," a girl said. "I trust older people's intuition."

Dylan looked up from his roll sheet. Lucy stood next to Otis. Today she had on a denim miniskirt embroidered with unicorns, a white T-shirt with a chicken saying, "Eat more veggies" on it, and a purple headband. She stared defiantly back at him, her hand on Otis's shoulder. "You ready for camp?"

"Yeah!" Otis reached out to fist bump Dylan. "Ready, Coach?"

"Give me a few more minutes to check people in. You're… um, you're early today." He couldn't resist glancing up at Lucy, who rolled her eyes in return. "Go run some laps with the guys who are here. I'll be there to lead stretches in a bit."

"Great!" Otis took off for the pitchers mound, calling out to new friends from yesterday.

Lucy watched him go. "I haven't seen him this happy in a while."

She sounded so sad, Dylan couldn't help asking, "Everything okay?"

"It's nothing." Like the snap of a Venus Fly Trap, Lucy's guard went up. "I'm going to hang in the stands until he's done."

"O-okay." He wanted to say more, but what? "I'll, um, I'll bring him to you."

She paused, one earbud already in. "That's not necessary."

"I know that." God, was she always this contrary? "I wanted to talk. About…last night."

"Whatever." She turned to go, shoulders slumped, and Dylan felt worse than before.

"Last night?" Nate perked up— Dylan had forgotten he was sitting there. "What about last night?"

"Nothing." Dylan picked up his pen as the next kid hopped out of a minivan. "Nothing at all."

Chapter Eight

The wind whistled through the stadium tunnel, making it nearly impossible to sew, so Lucy sat against the wall, staring at graffiti that said, "Despair." She snorted. People were so melodramatic sometimes.

Including her.

She'd walked up to registration, fully prepared to act cool, to push Dylan's buttons a bit. And she had—just not in the way she'd planned. What was it about this guy that made her feel both hot and cold, furious and hungry, sad and curious? Seriously, how many emotions could one girl's chest hold? And why was she trying to be something she wasn't? Did his opinion really matter that much?

She'd even dressed more girly than usual. Sure, the chicken shirt was a little out there, but a headband? For real?

She pulled it off her head and plaited her hair into pigtails. That made her feel better, more natural. Scrolling on her phone, she found the one song that made her laugh every time. *Space Unicorn* by Parry Gripp should be required listening at the start of every day. People would be less inclined to be snippy.

Lucy leaned her head against the wall and closed her eyes, letting all her happy music wash over her. She hadn't done this kind of forced cheer up for a long time, not since the week after Dad left, and it surprised her by working. A smile tugged at her mouth. Thinking about the kiss last night now seemed more funny—and damn hot—instead of crazy and embarrassing.

She was so busy singing to herself, she missed the first thunderclap. But the next fork of lightning burned through her eyelids, and she opened them to a sheet of water rolling down the ramp. Lucy ran up to the opening to the stands to see the guys herding the little ones into the dugout. Dylan was the last one out there, helping up a kid who'd fallen. He handed him off to one of his buddies before jogging around, looking for something.

Lucy started when his gaze met hers. He'd been checking out the stands, making sure she was under cover. Warmth spread through her chest, and she waved to let him know she was okay, before running down the ramp to hide out in the ladies' room until the storm was over.

The sun had come out by the time noon rolled around, and Lucy found Otis standing with the other boys waiting for rides. He bounded over to her. "We got to watch the last half of the state championship game. The real coach—the high school one—paused it to show off different things. Did you know Coach Dylan was the winning pitcher? He went extra innings!"

"I didn't know that." Lucy glanced at the players herding

the boys toward their cars. "You like him?"

"Coach Dylan? Yeah. He says I have a great arm for my age. Says I'll have his spot in six years." Otis's chest swelled with pride. "It's going to be the best camp ever."

"I'm glad." And she was. She caught Dylan's eye over the heads of the little leaguers and gave him a small nod. "Mind if we hang out a minute? Dyl—Coach Dylan wanted to talk to me a second."

"Okay."

Otis sat on a bench outside the fence and pulled out a book: *The Everything Kids' Baseball Book*. It didn't have a library binding and it looked new. Lucy sat beside him. "Where'd that come from?"

Otis glanced up. "Coach Dylan. He gave all the pitchers one."

Lucy's jaw dropped. "That's something."

Otis ignored her. He was totally engrossed. She'd never seen him willingly read, but maybe they'd been giving him the wrong kind of books. Funny how Dylan knew what he'd like.

Once the last kid—other than Otis—was gone, Dylan came over. Otis was still reading his book, although Lucy could tell he noticed his coach was nearby. She cleared her throat. "Can we take a quick walk?"

Dylan nodded. He looked tired, but his eyes were shining, despite the damp uniform clinging to his shoulders. Lucy had to look away.

"What are you humming?" he asked.

Lucy flushed. "Oh, I hum when I walk. I…didn't notice."

"You were really into it." He smiled. "Must be a song you like."

Yeah, Space Unicorn. *You know it? It's great.* Lucy shrugged. "Not sure. It could be anything. So, um, about last night."

He nodded, and his cheeks were pink, too. "I'm sorry I

yelled. I have no idea what happened to me. I'm usually more chill than that."

She cocked her head. "Maybe it was a sign you shouldn't be."

"Maybe, but I didn't have to be rude." He paused. "I'm not that guy. Usually."

They'd walked halfway down the foul line from first. Otis was still in view, barely, and Lucy could tell he was pretending to read. Her brother was *very* interested in what his sister did with his beloved Coach Dylan.

"And I'm not that girl." She laughed softly. "Wait, that's not true. My mom accuses me of being a hothead. She's probably right. But I didn't have to be rude, either. I have a problem with pushing buttons to see what happens."

"Is that why you kissed me?" he asked.

She raised an eyebrow. "I think *you* kissed *me.*"

"You started it." He swayed closer to her, mischief in his eyes. "I don't like to leave things unfinished."

"Oh, I could tell." Her pulse quickened, both from his nearness, and from curiosity. "Who hurt you?"

Surprise flitted across his features. He was closing down. "Nobody."

"Not true." Disappointed, she turned to walk back to Otis. "But when you're ready to share, I'll listen."

She left him there, wondering if he'd follow. After a second, he called, "What's with the chicken?"

She smiled, but didn't turn. "I'm a fan."

"Mom, I think Lucy scared Coach Dylan!" Otis burst through the front door of the shop before she could catch him. "Tell her to be nice!"

"For the tenth time, I didn't scare him. We were just

talking."

Otis rounded on her, his face stern. "Then why did he run off after you talked to him? I wanted to say bye."

Guilt clawed up Lucy's throat. "Maybe he had something to do."

Mom stopped putting away quilting supplies, giving a meaningful look to the three old ladies browsing fabric in the corner, then went to the back room. Otis and Lucy followed.

Mom took a seat at her sewing table. "Okay, what's this about? Lucy, were you messing with the coach?"

She always assumed it was Lucy's fault. "No." Well, *yes*, but not how anybody thought. "We were talking. I, um, saw him at the lake last night. That's all."

Mom's eyes widened, and the corner of her mouth turned up. "That's all?"

Otis pointed at Lucy. "See? I told you she was bothering him."

"Honey, I don't think this is quite what you imagined. It'll be okay." Mom reached out and caught him into a hug that he promptly squirmed out of. "Don't be jealous if Lucy talks to Coach Dylan. They're the same age, I think, so they have stuff in common."

Something like horror came over Otis's face. "Oh, no… no way, Lucy. You aren't going to date my coach."

Lucy threw up her hands. "Who said I was? We. Were. Talking. That's it."

Otis went on like he hadn't heard a word. "Then she'll break up with him over something stupid, like eating chicken nuggets, and he won't want to coach me anymore."

"Okay, first off, he's paid to coach you," Mom said. "Second, your sister is free to date any decent young man she chooses."

"There's no dating. None. I'm too busy for a guy right now, anyway. My projects aren't getting done with us arguing, either." Lucy stalked to her sewing chair and pulled the baby blanket out of her bag to finish the caterpillar. "I'm going to work."

She was starting to feel like she was in a box that was steadily becoming smaller, with no chance of fresh air. It was summer, and she hadn't had a single real day off yet. God, how'd she get here?

Stop stressing already. You have work to do.

She shoved her earbuds in and turned on her happy music as loud as she could, but it didn't drown out Otis's frown as he plunked into his beanbag chair to play video games.

Chapter Nine

Dylan

How did Lucy know he'd been hurt? Dylan sat in his car, hands on the steering wheel, without driving. She'd asked who hurt him…how'd she guess that? Had Serena, through their twisted grapevine of friends, found out and told her? Or was it simply that obvious?

His phone buzzed. Tristan. *Dude, I'm at Snaps for burgers. Where are you?*

Dylan blinked. Snaps, right. He was supposed to be at Snaps. God, this girl was unraveling him thread by thread. Lucy and her chicken shirt wouldn't leave his brain, and that was dangerous. Two days and he was already forgetting where he was supposed to be.

D: *Sorry, got held up. Coming.*

He started the car, pointed it in the direction of the restaurant, and drove. Lunch with his best friend was exactly what he needed to exorcize Lucy from his head.

When he got there, though, it wasn't just Tristan. Alyssa was there, too. Alyssa's smile was warm, kind, but he always felt a jolt of surprise when he saw her, a little zap of pain reminding him of the day he walked in on her and Tristan. He managed to smile back, as he took the seat next to her.

"Okay, tell me who she is." Alyssa gave him a French fry from the basket on the table. "Who's the girl who thawed you out?"

"Thawed me out? That's a new one." Dylan chewed the fry, giving her a puzzled look.

Alyssa flashed a smile that would melt most guys. "Your nickname *is* Iceman. Finding a girl who's less structured would be good for you."

"How do you even know about this?" Dylan turned to Tristan. "Why did you tell her? You knew she'd give me hell about it."

"That's exactly why I told her." Tristan ducked as Dylan's napkin soared at his head. "I'm tired of you looking tired."

"I don't want to talk about it." Dylan swiped the basket of fries and crammed three in his mouth.

"Avoiding it won't change a thing," Alyssa said. She leaned against the table, a strand of curly hair falling over her shoulder. "We just want you to be happy."

"I am happy. I'm focused, and my pitching is really great right now. Stop worrying about me."

Tristan gave Alyssa a "see what I mean?" look and she shook her head. "He'll be all right. I have hope."

All this matchmaking was making his stomach hurt. "I'm not feeling well. Think I'll go."

He threw a five on the table and left before they could call him back.

"Dylan, is that you?" Mom's voice came from the laundry room at the back of the house. "I have clean workout stuff for you to carry upstairs."

No avoiding her, then. She'd know something was wrong, and he wasn't ready to talk. Sighing, he carried today's workout clothes to the hamper next to the washer—his dirty gear wasn't supposed to make it to his room—and took the load of laundry from her. Under Armor shirts, Nike shorts and socks, baseball pants. All of it familiar and smelling like fabric softener. The top layer was still warm.

"Thanks, Mom." He turned to go upstairs, but she called him back.

"What's wrong? You've been off for days. You aren't sick or hurt and hiding it are you?" Mom gave him a quick once over. "Or is it something else?"

Just like magic—his mom always knew somehow. "I'm fine. Just tired. Those little leaguers don't slow down." He smiled. "Ever."

"Oh, I remember having a nine-year-old boy. After your sister, you were like an alien with an endless battery supply." Mom squeezed his arm. "I don't like seeing you stressed out. Maybe if you worked on some college applications now, got ahead, you'd…"

Dylan froze. "I thought we agreed I'd hold off until the scouts took a look at me."

Mom forced a smile. "Yes, but it's good to be prepared." She raised an eyebrow at his sour look. "Honey, Dad and I would feel better if you went to college first, rather than straight to the minors. That way you'd have something to fall back on, in case things don't work out."

"Uncle Rick went straight to the minors, and things turned out just fine for him." Dylan's pulse started to pound in his temple. "Or is it that you and Dad don't think I'm good enough to make it?"

"Oh, Dylan, it's not that." Mom reached for him, but he took a step back. "We want what's best for you. You have a three-point-five GPA and take honors classes. I thought… maybe you'd want to continue your education."

"I have a plan, Mom. There's time for college after the minors if I don't make it." He turned to avoid her concerned expression. "But that's plan B, and I'm not ready to think about it yet."

Once Dylan was upstairs, he put his clothes away methodically, not really thinking about it. He felt like the walls were closing in around him, especially when he saw a stack of college applications on his desk. The sticky note on top read: *Just think about it, son. –Dad.*

Dylan paced his room, wishing he could rage against the sky. Everybody thought they knew what was right for him, from his friends to his family. They didn't understand. No one did—how he woke up every morning looking ahead. How he studied major league pitchers to see what he needed to work on next. How much of his life was pointing in one direction. And sometimes they weren't even willing to listen.

He snatched up his phone to text Uncle Rick on his ranch. *Can I come live with you? Just for a few weeks? I'll work cattle, whatever it takes.*

R: *Whoa, where'd that come from?*

D: *Everyone's bent on deciding stuff for me, and you don't. I need someone who understands.*

R: *I don't think moving eighty minutes from the nearest store is really what you want. How about I come up for a few days instead? I've been meaning to visit.*

Dylan stared at his phone. Would having Rick here help? Maybe. If he could talk to his parents, they might listen. *Okay.*

Dylan's stomach rumbled. He still hadn't eaten lunch, but he wasn't sure he much felt like it. Coach would nag him to death if he found out Dylan had skipped a meal, but whatever. The chaos in his head needed to settle before he tried to eat.

A soft meow by the cracked bedroom door alerted him to Huck's presence. Their tabby rarely showed up in Dylan's room. Today, he must've sensed Dylan needed company and decided to pity him. Huck hopped onto Dylan's bed and bumped his head against Dylan's hand.

"Hey, buddy." Dylan scratched Huck under the chin and behind his ears, and the cat purred in delight. "Nice of you to visit."

Despite Huck's calming presence, something kept nagging at Dylan. Why did everything feel like it was in black and white? Like he was living in the beginning of *The Wizard of Oz* waiting for the Technicolor to begin. His life had boiled down to "step one, step two, step three." Most of the time, that suited him just fine. Today, though…all he wanted to do was run. To let it all go, drop the discipline, for one freaking day. No one he knew would even believe he could feel that way. He was "Iceman" to his friends, and an unreasonable son to his parents.

Except…there was one person who didn't seem to live by the same rules. Hell, she didn't seem to live by *any* rules. And every time Dylan saw her, a tiny flicker of life flared up in his chest. Maybe Lucy could spark some anarchy in his heart.

On the other hand, this could swerve out of control pretty fast. He couldn't let it become a thing. He wanted to see her, but he'd have to be careful. He didn't have time for a relationship. Or even for the chance of one.

Just for today. That's all. One afternoon, a little voice wheedled in his head. *One time won't hurt.*

Blowing out a breath, he texted Tristan. *Do you have the roster for the campers?*

T: *Yeah, why?*

Dylan swallowed down his nerves. *Is Otis's emergency contact Lucy?*

T: *Uh, hang on.*

The pause seemed to drag on forever. Finally: *It's his mom, but there's a second number, a cell. I bet that's her.*

D: *Can you send it?*

Ten seconds later Tristan answered. *About time you made a move.*

Dylan sank down on his mattress, staring at the number and hoping he wasn't about to make a giant mistake. But maybe a giant mistake was exactly what he needed.

Chapter Ten

Lucy was tying off the end of the caterpillar's top hat when her phone buzzed. She looked up to find the windows dark with another incoming storm, and Otis on his stomach, watching the end of a *Teenage Mutant Ninja Turtles* movie. "Where's Mom?"

"She went to pick up a pizza. I'm hungry." He pointed at her phone. "That's been buzzing a while now."

She'd been listening to her music, intent on finishing this project, so she must have missed it. Serena was probably herding the chickens in early and needed help.

Lucy picked up her phone and almost dropped it.

D: *Lucy? It's Dylan.*

D: *Um, Tristan gave me your number. Off the camp roster.*

D: *Yeah, probably shouldn't have mentioned that. Now I look like a stalker.*

D: *I swear I'm not a stalker.*

D: *Sorry, I must be bothering you. I'll go now.*

The texts had been rolling in for an hour. Otis must've seen the shocked look on her face, because he scrambled out of the playroom. "It's not something about Dad is it?"

His voice went up an octave at the last bit, and Lucy relaxed her features. "No, it's nothing. Just…a surprise text from…a friend. That's all."

"Oh." Otis acted like it was nothing. "Tell Serena to quit texting you dirty jokes, then."

Lucy laughed, feeling awkward. "Will do. Enjoy the movie."

Once the DVD player started again, she unlocked her phone and typed. *I wasn't ignoring you. Just got these.*

She chewed her lip, wondering what Dylan wanted. *Everything okay?*

It took a minute for him to respond. *I…don't know. Look, you want to get some coffee?*

Did she? She stared at the newly finished blanket, thinking about the orders for custom work on a wedding dress, two more blankets, and a baby's christening gown she'd yet to start. Serena also might call at any minute, begging her for help at the farm. And she couldn't leave Otis by himself. Or the shop unattended, for that matter.

Still, there was some unfinished business with this guy. She really didn't have time for him, but…didn't she need a break? Could she even take one? Because, she couldn't help wondering what Dylan really wanted. A little tug in her middle urged her to say yes, even though it was impossible.

The bells over the front door rang, and Mom came in, windblown and laughing. "Whew. It's a gale out there. Who wants pizza?"

Lucy froze. Okay, so two of her excuses were taken care of with Mom's return. But the storm was a problem. Wondering if she was being stupid, she texted Serena. *How are my girls?*

> S: *Everyone's in the hen houses, waiting on the rain. We fed them early, in case you were planning to come out.*

It was like the universe was telling her something. She glanced at the blanket. She *had* finished a project. Didn't that call for a little celebration? She'd have to work late tonight on the dress, but it was just coffee, right?

She texted Dylan: *Sure. How about now?*

> D: *Fine with me, but there's another storm coming.*

> L: *So?*

It took another full minute for him to respond. *Green Bean in twenty?*

Now Lucy smiled. *No, the North Marina Coffee Shop. I'll be there in fifteen.*

> D: *Is this a test?*

> L: *Yes. And you strike me as a guy who likes to pass them.*

> D: …

> D: …

> D: *Okay. See you in fifteen.*

Lucy grinned at her phone. "I'm going out."

Mom looked up from the pizza. Otis had a paper plate out for more. "In this weather?"

"It's not *that* bad." Lucy gave her an innocent smile. "I'll be fine."

Her mother glanced at the windows, then back at her. "Okay, hurry wherever you're going, though, and stay there until it passes."

Lucy crossed her fingers behind her back. "Sure thing."

The lake had whitecaps by the time she dashed into the coffee shop. Thunder rumbled and lightning flashed almost constantly. It wasn't raining—yet—but thick, gray clouds boiled over the edge of the lake. She'd resolved not to feel guilty—not much anyway—about leaving her work for later, and she was glad she'd taken the break. Storms like this made Lucy feel alive, free. But her grin wasn't because of the storm. No, a Porsche crossover had just pulled into the marina's lot, and when the door opened, Dylan hopped out.

"Nice car," she said over a crack of thunder. "Is it yours?"

"Was my mom's, but it's mine now." He looked uncomfortable. "Why did you want to meet out here?"

The marina diner had decent coffee, but you could have a better cup at Green Bean in town. He knew something was up. "We're having coffee to go."

He looked outside. "And where are we going after that?"

She smiled. "You'll see."

He ordered a black coffee before asking her what she wanted. Lucy shook her head…this guy couldn't even have fun with coffee. "Quad latte."

Dylan looked at her sidelong. "Caffeine much?"

"The elixir of life, my friend." She nudged his hip with hers, biting back a smile when he turned red. "Black coffee is boring."

"I like boring."

"Really? I couldn't tell." Lucy grabbed her drink from the counter and took Dylan's free hand. If that shocked him, he didn't show it. His hand was big, nearly swallowing hers. She kind of liked that. "Are you waterproof?"

"Should I be afraid to answer that?"

She let him go long enough to fling open the door, letting the wind gust inside. "Probably."

She led him down the gravel path behind the marina to the trail around the lake. Fat drops of rain fell here and there, promising a deluge soon, but she figured they'd make it.

"Really, though," Dylan shouted over the wind. "Where are we going?"

She pointed. "There's a shelter nearby. Not far now."

Lucy knew there wouldn't be anyone crazy enough to use the picnic shelter, and it was empty when they arrived. It was large enough that the center of the concrete floor, next to one of the metal tables, would stay completely dry. She'd whiled away a lot of storms out here reading when she needed to be alone. She pulled Dylan under the roof just as the sky opened up and the rain became a curtain around the shelter.

"Ta-da!" She grinned and led him to the center table, patting the bench beside her.

"We're in a metal building. In a thunderstorm." He looked around, eyebrow raised. "Sitting at a *metal* table."

She shrugged and pointed at the flagpole barely visible outside. "That's taller and has a lightning rod on it. Besides, it's cloud-to-cloud lightning. Didn't you notice?"

Dylan sank down like the bench. "No, but okay."

"Dylan, look at me." When his eyes met hers, skeptical, she sighed. "You texted me for a reason. I don't know what it is, but I'm taking a guess. You're feeling stifled, and you called the only crazy person you know. Am I right?"

He gave her a grudging smile. "How'd you know?"

The way he said it, like he was tired of trying so hard, made her chest ache. "I can see the cracks. You're one bad day away from flipping out." Lucy drew her legs up to sit crisscross on the bench. There had to be a way to shake him loose from this funk. "First step is to live like today is all there is. Human beings were built to take risks. So, get comfy and forget the possibility of electrocution."

He relaxed slightly. "What's step two?"

She waved a hand. "A lesson for another day. Don't rush me."

He laughed. "Okay, sensei. So…we just listen to the rain?"

"Not exactly." She had him…and a wicked smile spread across her face. *This could be fun.* "When's the last time you played truth or dare?"

Oh, the look on his face. It was priceless. "Not since fifth grade. Why?"

So much suspicion. He was right to be suspicious. Keeping him off-kilter made her heart beat faster. Twisted, but true. "We play."

"I…I thought we were just going to talk." He held up his paper cup. "Have coffee."

"We are. We're just doing it my way." Lucy reached out and patted his arm, and her eyebrows shot up when she felt his biceps. There were perks to hanging out with baseball players after all. Her hand lingered on his arm, and he bit back a smirk. Uh huh…he might be stuck in a rut, but Dylan Dennings knew what his assets were, and he probably knew how to use them.

Heat flushed Lucy's face. Being in near dark made this feel *way* more intimate.

They sat there, staring at each other until, finally, Dylan cleared his throat and looked away.

Right. The game.

She released his arm and folded her hands in her lap. The light was growing dim outside, but not quite enough to make the lights kick on, so his face was shadowed. "So which one do you want? Truth? Or dare?"

Chapter Eleven

Lucy's smile was bright and quick in the dim light. Was this another test? Was playing the game a dare in and of itself? He should say no, but he was tired of doing things as expected. Besides, when she touched his arm, he'd forgotten why he'd been in a bad mood to begin with. It also left him with the desire to impress her. He wasn't sure how to do that, but he'd try.

Straightening his spine, he said, "Truth."

"Okay, and if you don't want to answer, you can choose the dare." She settled herself on the bench. "Who hurt you?"

"Starting off hot, huh?" He picked at his fingernails. "A girl. She's…she's dating my best friend. It's not like she ever said yes to me, but it hurt."

"Understandable." Lucy's tone was kind, and her quicksilver smile faded to something more sympathetic, but not pitying. Like she understood. "Your turn. I want truth."

"Fair enough." He pretended to consider, even though he

already knew what to ask. "Did you tell Serena I'm cute?"

Lucy looked at the ground and laughed softly. "Yes. Your turn."

She *did* think he was cute. The back of his neck grew warm. "Truth."

She sat up and smiled. It was an evil smile. "What are you afraid of?"

"Spiders."

"No." She gave him a stern look. "What are you *afraid* of?"

Dylan sank back into himself a little bit, his stomach rolling over. "Failure."

She reached out to squeeze his forearm, nodding. "Bingo. We have some work to do, then. Failure is how you learn. Do you know how many pieces I had to rip apart before I really learned?"

"Learned what?" he asked.

"This counts as my turn."

"Aw, man." He swung a leg over to straddle the bench. They weren't too comfortable, and the rain was deafening on the metal roof. "Fine."

"Needlepoint. I'm really good, actually. Doing work from patterns was too…stifling, so I decided to do custom designs. I sucked at first and worked to get better." She pointed a finger at him. "But I don't get upset if I mess up a piece. I just try again. Your turn."

"Truth."

"Dylan…you're so cautious." She blew a raspberry at him. "Why did you buy my brother the book?"

What a weird question. "Because I loved it when I was his age and thought my little leaguers would enjoy it. Besides, kids that age don't read enough."

Lucy froze. He had no idea what he said to cause a reaction, but she was perfectly still. "Dare."

Whoa. He hadn't even thought that far ahead. "Um, stand on the table and sing 'Itsy, Bitsy, Spider.'"

She climbed onto the table, smirking. "I thought you were afraid of spiders."

He laughed. "Less talking, more singing."

She did as she was told, adding goofy dance moves, then pointed at him. He knew what she was asking, and if he wanted this game to go on—which he *really* did—he had to say it. He had to leave the safe spaces behind. He'd wanted to feel alive, to loosen up. Here was his chance.

"Dare."

She squealed and clapped her hands together. "Run with me in the rain."

He glanced at the sheet of water pouring over the edge of the shelter's roof. "What?"

She hopped off the table and stood toe-to-toe with him. He fought an urge to wrap his arms around her. "We're going to run in the rain."

"We are?"

But Lucy was already backing up. With a wink, she stepped off the shelter's edge with a squeak.

Dylan laughed. How, exactly, did this girl's mind work? Shaking his head, he pulled his keys, wallet, and phone out of his pocket, then dashed out into the rain to find her.

She was dancing. In the rain. Whooping like mad and twirling in circles. Her chicken T-shirt was plastered to her chest, and her face was upturned to catch drops in her mouth. His feet gained a mind of their own, drawing him closer and closer, and he had a hard time keeping his eyes fixed on her face, especially when he noticed the hot pink bra showing through her wet shirt. God, this girl was crazy, but…he could get used to it.

She stopped and grinned at him over her shoulder, her wet pigtails clinging to her neck, "See, it's not so bad. Tilt your head back. Stop trying to be in control—because you can't be, not out here."

Dylan's chest hitched, and he felt short of breath, like he'd run out here rather than strolled. Tearing his eyes away from Lucy, he tipped his face up to the rain. The droplets pelted him, and he had to close his eyes. The rain tasted metallic as it landed on his tongue. Slowly, the knot inside him released, came undone.

Lucy slipped her hand into his. "Better?"

He ran a finger along her palm, smiling up at the rain when he felt her shiver. "Yeah. Much better."

Dylan crept in through the back door. Mom was in the kitchen, preparing dinner, and he could hear Dad on the phone. They'd never understand the damp clothes or bleary eyes, so he had to sneak in. He and Lucy had played in the rain—nothing more than that—for more than an hour before the storm blew over and they decided to go home. He couldn't remember the last time he'd had so much fun. His leather car seat was slick and the floorboards were soaked, but they'd dry.

When his dad paced into his study and Mom stuck her head into the fridge for something, Dylan dashed through the kitchen and living room to the stairs. He couldn't explain the wet hair, either, so he started up the shower. Just in time, too, because his dad came clomping upstairs.

"Dylan, Uncle Rick called. He's coming up Saturday."

So Rick had gone through with it after all. "Oh…okay, thanks. It'll be good to see him."

"Yeah. When you're done with your shower, come down. I think dinner's almost ready."

Dylan let out a sigh of relief. Things were starting to come together. "I will."

Despite that, Dylan didn't go shower. He decided he had a new plan, in addition to The Plan. He wasn't sure he could manage both at the same time, but he wanted to try.

He wanted to make Lucy smile.

The next morning, Dylan stirred, wondering why his alarm hadn't gone off. His eyes flew open. Eight.

"Oh my God." He leapt out of bed and ran to his closet, throwing on the first T-shirt and pair of shorts he saw. He never forgot to set his alarm and should've been up ninety minutes ago. The campers would start showing up in half an hour.

He streaked through the house, shoving a baseball cap on his head and grabbing an apple on his way to the garage. Mom waved a confused good-bye. Dad was already long gone.

He took off for the ball field, panic making him lean on the accelerator a little too much, especially after he got caught waiting on a train to pass. He was half a mile from the school when red and blue lights filled his rearview mirror.

Cursing under his breath, Dylan pulled into a convenience store parking lot and closed his eyes. This couldn't be happening. It was eight-twenty—he would be late.

The cop took his time before climbing out of his car and approaching Dylan's vehicle. "Son, you were doing ten over back there."

"I'm sorry." Dylan put his hands on the steering wheel and stared through the windshield. His face burned, and his stomach threatened to launch the apple onto the dashboard. "I…woke up late."

"It happens, but you need to be more careful. License and registration."

Dylan produced the documents, then sat back to wait.

Twenty-five minutes later, he showed up to the ballpark with a ticket for a hundred-twenty dollars and a lecture ringing in his ears. He'd have to take Defensive Driving online now, on top of everything else, to keep the ticket off his insurance record. Tristan frowned when Dylan jogged onto the field.

"Where've you been? It's almost nine."

"Woke up late, got a ticket." Dylan dragged a basket of baseballs over to the mound and sent his pitchers out for their morning jog.

"But, Coach Dylan, we already went," one of the boys said. The others nodded.

God, he was so late. "Could you run one more? You never can get too much conditioning."

They grumbled but did as he asked. Tristan raised an eyebrow. "You okay? You're a little…scatterbrained today."

"I'm fine. I just need a second to focus."

Tristan kept staring at him. "You ever talk to Lucy? Is something up?"

"Yes and…not sure." He looked at the knot of pitchers jogging around the field. "Speaking of which, Otis isn't here yet."

Tristan pointed at the lot. "There he is."

The kid was flat out running in from the parking lot, Lucy jogging to keep up. "Otis! You forgot your glove!"

Otis skidded to a halt next to the check-in table. "Can that count as my warm up, Coach Dylan?"

Dylan nodded. "Go to the mound with the rest of the boys. I'll see you in a second."

Lucy came, huffing and puffing, her hair falling out of her braid and creases on her cheek. "The power went out last night, and none of our alarms went off."

"Sounds familiar." Dylan held out a hand. "We need to get started. Can I have the glove?"

The words came out sharp enough to cut. Having a shit

morning wasn't an excuse for being an asshole, but nothing felt right. Too chaotic or something.

Lucy's eyebrow rose, and she handed over the glove without a word. Before he could choke out an apology, she spun on her heel and marched to the parking lot. Dylan's teeth ground together.

Determined to turn this morning around, he called to his campers, "Everyone pair up for catching practice. Hustle!"

Maybe if he found some sense of control out here, everything would be just fine.

Chapter Twelve

LUCY

Lucy stomped into her mom's shop. *Of all the infuriating…*it wasn't her fault that the alarm clocks were blinking midnight when Otis shook her awake. Dylan had no right to be so… so…judgmental. Hadn't she gotten through to him last night in the rain? She'd felt a flare between them. Outrageous, because it sounded impossible, but her nerve endings had lit up more than once when she'd grabbed his hand or touched his arm. They'd had so much fun, too. Maybe that was the problem…maybe Dylan was allergic to fun.

Didn't matter. She had a ton of work to do, and no time to spend worrying about Dylan.

But you still want to, a little voice piped up.

She shook that thought off. Too much on her plate to listen to little voices or dwell on sparks when you touched a guy's hand. Her needle was waiting, and it wasn't nearly as moody as a certain pitcher she knew.

The ladies in Mom's quilting class looked up briefly

when Lucy strode through the front room. Most waved in greeting—she'd known half of them her entire life…like an entire squad of grandmas ready to spoil her rotten. She smiled at all of them, forcing herself to be warm and welcoming as she breezed by.

Mom was in the back, sorting through quilting pieces, with a pinched expression on her face. Lucy's stomach turned to ice. *Not now. Not today. I can't handle anything else right now…*

But her mother was moving like she was swimming in Jell-O, careful not to turn her head too much. Lucy went to her and put a hand on her arm. "Mom?"

Mom looked up slowly, squinting under the shop's fluorescent lights. The laugh lines around her eyes were deep, and a furrow had dug itself in between her eyebrows. "Hey, honey."

"Migraine?" At her mother's nod, Lucy took the quilt pieces out of her hands. "I'll run the class. You need to lie down." Work would have to wait. Until when, Lucy didn't know…but she'd manage. Somehow. Who needed sleep, anyway?

"I'll be fine." The words were weak. "You have all those new orders…"

Yes, she did. The black wedding gown, in particular, would be a lot of work. The bride wanted a punk rose-vine, complete with thorns, along the hem. Goth-bride for the win. "I have plenty of time," she lied. "Go rest."

Mom nodded, winced, then headed to the back of the shop, a testament to how bad it was. Usually she powered through, but every couple of months, a migraine hit her so hard she could barely function. Lucy hated seeing her this way. It seemed like since Dad had deployed, the headaches were getting worse and more frequent, and without him here, Lucy had to be in charge. It scared her. What if she messed everything up? Mom couldn't handle much stress, so Lucy couldn't afford to screw up, not even a little.

She took a deep breath, fighting back tears. It would be okay. It had to be. *Fake it until you make it, girl. You got this.*

Lucy waited until the playroom door shut before announcing, "Greetings, campers! I'll be your host today."

"Aw, Lucy-girl!" Mrs. Jennings, her favorite regular at the store, said. "Aren't we in luck."

"You are, because I'm going to…" Lucy paused for dramatic effect. "Teach you to use the new embroidery machine!"

Eight gray-haired ladies cheered like she'd offered them a gin and tonic, paired with a date with Robert Redford. The little things made them happy. She rubbed her hands together, feeling a little better about how the morning would turn out. Time to work some magic.

Lucy rang up Mrs. Jennings's purchases, then stopped to stretch. Crazy morning, but they'd loved the new machine. One woman planned to monogram everything her granddaughter owned, or so it sounded. Lucy smiled, pleased. That would turn into some nice revenue for the store.

Mom still hadn't emerged from the playroom. It had been more than two hours, now. A prickle of fear rose on the back of Lucy's neck as she headed for the back of the shop. Mom's migraines could be bad and fairly regular, but usually not terrible.

Usually…but not always.

"Mom?" Lucy asked, a tremor in her voice. She knocked on the playroom door. "Mom, you okay?"

A soft groan made her heart lurch, and she pushed the door open. The trash can, smelling of sick, sat next to the sofa, and her mom flung an arm over her eyes at the sliver of light arcing into the room from the shop. "Don't…know…"

Lucy closed the door and made her way to the sofa in the dim light. She pulled Mom's arm away from her eyes. Her left eyelid was doing its twitchy dance, and her eyes were glazed. This was a bad one. Maybe one of the worst.

"We need to get you to the doctor." Lucy helped her mother sit up, trying not to gag at the vomit stench in the room. "I'm going for your sunglasses."

"What about Otis?" Mom's speech was slurred and her hands shook.

What *about* Otis? Given what she was seeing, Lucy didn't have a choice as to where she was needed, but she still felt torn in two. God, she wished Dad were home. He could've taken care of Mom, leaving Lucy to watch the shop and her little brother. "I'll text a few of his friends' moms. Someone can bring him…"

Lucy's palms started to sweat. Bring Otis *where*? He couldn't stay home by himself, and no telling how long they'd be at the doctor. "Um, I'll figure that part out."

Mom started to nod, winced. "Help me up."

It took several minutes to walk her to the car, and a few more to close up the shop with a cheery sign that said, *Closed, but we'll be back soon!* By the time Lucy made it to the Jeep, her T-shirt was stuck to her back from the summer heat. She ran the A/C until she saw her mother shivering next to her, then turned it off and rolled down her window, resigning herself to the sweat.

Mom's neurologist was thirty minutes away, but she knew he'd prefer to see her. Dr. Westfield was one of the best in the Dallas area, and he always wanted his patients to come straight to him during a bad attack, rather than the primary doctor. At the last stoplight on the way out of Suttonville, she texted Otis: *Squirt— Mom's bad off. Can Joey or Max give you a ride home? Sorry about this. I'll text once I'm at Dr. W's.*

Lucy stuck to the speed limit the whole way there,

sneaking worried glances at her mother. Mom had her head in her hands and eye scrunched tightly shut. The fact that she wasn't remarking on Lucy's driving, or asking about her projects, or...hell, or even *talking* at all was probably the scariest thing.

Glad the car had Bluetooth, she called the doctor's office and, as Lucy had thought, they said to bring Mom straight there. It was so strange, being the one in charge. The one making the phone calls and the frantic drive to the doctor. She was only seventeen, but right now she felt like she was twice that.

Lucy swallowed against a sob rising in her throat. It would be okay.

It had to be.

When they made it to Dr. Westfield's building, Mom could barely move. Her gait was jerky, and she weaved when she walked. Lucy finally had to hang firmly onto her mother's arm to guide her inside. Inside...oh, thank God for over-air-conditioned buildings. Lucy felt a little guilty at enjoying that as her mother shivered in the elevator, but not a lot.

The receptionist jumped up when they came in and opened the door to the back, bypassing the waiting patients, some of whom clucked in disapproval. Lucy almost bared her teeth and hissed back. None of *them* was semi-conscious and deathly pale. They could wait, and to hell with their disapproving stares.

"Oh, dear," the receptionist said, glancing back at them as she led them to an empty exam room. "This is a bad one, isn't it?"

"The worst," Lucy said. "I've never seen her this bad."

"You're a good girl, taking care of your mother."

Maybe so, but Lucy's knees were shaking. She felt like a fraud accepting the praise when she was barely keeping it together herself. The little box she'd felt closing in around her was getting smaller by the day.

A nurse stuck her head in, took one look at Mom, and left. The receptionist nodded. "She's going to triage your mother to next-patient status. Hang in there a bit longer, Mrs. Foster. We'll fix you right up."

Mom mumbled something like a thank you and Lucy sank into the chair next to the exam table, wishing she could lie down, too. The nurse bustled back inside, dimming the lights, giving Mom a warm blanket, taking her temperature and blood pressure—both too high.

"Dr. Westfall will be here shortly." The nurse glanced at Lucy's mother. "We have her shots ready to go as soon as he gives the word."

Lucy nodded, tired. The experimental treatment, a specialty of this particular neurologist, had been a miracle, but it wasn't a cure. There would be more days like this. More days where she'd have to balance school, work, the shop, her brother, and Mom. Serena and the hens, and all the other things she wanted to do, had to wait.

A tear fought through her determined calm and slid down her cheek. *I want my dad.*

She dashed the tear away with the back of her hand, angry. It couldn't be helped. The Army didn't worry about such things. And a lieutenant colonel in the reserves didn't have any control over when—or where—he had to go. If the Army called, he had to take leave from his job at Texas Instruments and go wherever he was ordered.

Lucy closed her eyes. This too would pass. She wasn't easily defeated, but it was hard not to wallow. Just a little. Because she'd have to be strong for—

Her heart shot into her throat...she'd completely forgotten her brother. Lucy snatched her phone out of her purse. A single text from Otis: *It's okay. I found a ride.*

But with who?

Chapter Thirteen

DYLAN

Otis helped Dylan put away all the equipment as the other boys slowly disappeared into minivans and SUVs. Ten minutes after the pickup time, he was the only kid left at camp. Dylan scanned the parking lot, half afraid to see Lucy there. He'd been pretty rude this morning, irritated mostly at himself, but taking it out on her. Would she be willing to stick around so he could apologize?

Only one way to find out—he had to try. Even if his stomach was doing backflips.

"Any idea where your sister is?" he asked Otis.

The kid frowned. "She runs late a lot."

"This is *really* late," Dylan said, wondering if this was some kind of punishment for how he'd acted this morning. But, no, Lucy was too overprotective of her brother to leave him hanging. Something was wrong. "Maybe she left you a message?"

"Oh!" Otis took off for his equipment bag, having to

unpack his bats, a second glove, and a towel, before wrestling his phone free. That made Dylan laugh. His bag had always been orderly, from the time he was seven or eight. The other guys had poked fun at him for it, mainly because their bags looked more like Otis's disaster.

"Um, Coach Dylan?" Otis chewed on his lip. "She's not coming."

Dylan's eyebrows shot up. "What? She can't leave you here, man."

"No, it's not her fault. I should've checked sooner." Otis's lip trembled, and Dylan realized he was chewing on it to hold back tears. "My mom...she's sick. Lucy had to drive her to the doctor."

Okay, that didn't sound good. Mrs. Foster had to be very sick for Lucy to drop everything and leave Otis hanging like this. "Do you know when they'll be back?"

"No." A fat tear escaped Otis's eye. "S-sorry. I'm a big baby."

"You aren't. Anyone would be upset when their mom is sick." Dylan sighed. "Want to go to lunch? We could eat and figure out what to do next."

Otis's expression brightened so much it was comical. "Lunch? With you?"

"Sure, why not? Do you like Dolly's?" That was the drive-in everyone in town went to, and it had enough greasy food and ice cream to delight any nine-year-old. "I'll buy."

"I love Dolly's. It's my favorite." Otis was already texting. "I'm telling Lucy I have a ride." He gave Dylan a cagey look. "So she won't worry."

Just what did you text there, Otis? "Lucy, Coach Dylan is buying me lunch...nah-nah-nah-nah-nah-nah!" Complete with tongue-sticking-out emoji most likely. Dylan swallowed a laugh. "Good plan. Grab your gear— I'm starving."

"Me, too!"

Otis chattered the whole way to the car, whistling when he saw the Porsche. "And I thought my dad's Jeep was cool. This is awesome."

"You mean Lucy's Jeep?" That was what she drove, right?

"Not Lucy's. My dad's in the Army reserves. He got called up, so he's letting her drive it. I think she hopes he'll buy her a car when he comes home." Otis deflated a little. "Whenever that will be."

Dylan waited for Otis to climb into the passenger seat and buckle up before walking around to his side. Their dad was in the military? And gone? No wonder Lucy had to take care of her mom on the fly—they didn't have backup. Some of her flightiness fell into place. It was hard to focus when you were pulled in a thousand directions.

Dylan started the car and drove more carefully than usual, having a kid on board. Otis acted like a puppy on a ride, his face pressed against the window, watching the world go by. He had to have ridden this route a dozen or more times, but he acted like he'd never seen it. Dylan found himself smiling every time he glanced at Otis. He was a mix of Dylan's and Lucy's best qualities: focused and wanting to succeed, but enjoying the trip.

Dylan's chest ached. If things had been different, if *he'd* been different, wired in another way, he could've been this curious, hardworking, earnest kid. You couldn't unlearn things, though, so all he could do was appreciate Otis for what he was and take care of him until his family came home.

Dolly's was hopping when they pulled in. Dylan ordered burgers, fries, onion rings, and a chocolate shake, grinning when Otis's eyes grew huge.

"That's a lot of food," he said. "Can you really eat that much?"

"Some of it is for you." Dylan pointed at Otis's stomach. "There's room in there."

"Probably, but not as much as you." Otis settled happily in his seat. "Coach Dylan?"

"Yeah?"

"Do you like my sister?"

Dylan blinked. He'd forgotten how blunt kids were. "Um...she's nice."

Otis let out a hefty, dramatic sigh and jammed his ball cap harder onto his head. "Not like that. Like...*like* like."

It took Dylan a second to decipher that. "I...I just met her, Otis."

"Please don't go out with her."

Dylan froze. "Why not?"

"Because Lucy's Lucy, and you're you." Otis's tone was firm, like that made complete sense. "And you're *my* Coach."

A hint of jealousy, but some concern, too. "I'm not saying I'll go out with her..." *Again.* "But, even if we did, I'd still be your coach."

"Lucy's a little crazy." Otis said it with the vague fondness and annoyance that only younger brothers could produce. Dylan knew that tone well— He'd called his own sister crazy more than once. "If she makes you mad, you won't want to be my coach anymore."

"It doesn't work like that." Dylan scrubbed a hand through his hair, beginning to understand where all this was coming from. "Otis, I promise to be your coach as long as I can, no matter what. And when I leave for the minors, maybe your dad will be back to catch for you."

"Maybe." The kid's huge brown eyes were full of a loneliness unfair in a nine-year-old boy.

Dylan recognized that loneliness, and it sucked. "Hey, I have an idea. Do you know when Lucy will be back?"

Otis shook his head, looking curious. "Why?"

"Because I have a friend who works at Swing Away, the batting cages on route 27. We could hit balls for a while."

Otis's face split in a huge grin. "Really? I never get to go to the cages." He bounced in his seat. "Let's go!"

"Dude, we have to eat first." Dylan pointed at the carhop balancing a tray full of food. "Your body needs fuel to perform. Remember that."

Otis nodded, as if that was the best advice *ever*. "I will."

Dylan almost laughed, "All right, then. Eat up."

"Center your weight a little more," Dylan said, adjusting Otis's back foot. "Otherwise you'll lose momentum."

"He needs a different bat," a girl said outside the cage.

Dylan hid a grin. "Otis, I think you're about to get some coaching from the Suttonville Sentinels' secret weapon."

The kid lowered his bat, eyebrows raised, and turned. "Ooooh, you're Alyssa Kaplan."

Alyssa turned an incredulous look on Dylan. Just a few days ago, her brilliant green eyes would've left him weak in the knees...and a little pissy. Today, though, he noticed the sting was gone. "What?"

"Are you guys seriously creating a legend about me out there?" Alyssa put her hands on her hips. "Don't believe a word they say, kiddo. I was a decent hitter and a good pitcher when I played softball, but I'm not superhuman."

Otis peered at her. "Yes, but everyone knows how you helped Coach Tristan with his swing."

Alyssa mouthed, "*Coach Tristan?*" then laughed. "That I did. And *you* need a two-and-a-quarter bat, not a two-and-five-eighths."

"But the high schools use two-and-five-eighths," Otis said, shooting Dylan a look that clearly asked why they thought Alyssa was an expert. Dylan smirked back and waited.

"Because you need a lighter weight bat. It will help you

work on distance, speed, and bat control. The five-eighths is too big for you right now. Practice with the smaller barrel, and when you grow an inch or two, move back up."

She went to the supply closet across from cage 8, where they'd been hitting, and returned with an aluminum bat that had seen better days. "It's not pretty, but it'll do."

Otis looked at the bat like it might bite him. Dylan rolled his eyes and opened the cage door to take it from her. "Thanks."

"No problem." She cocked her head. "Who's the little guy, anyway?"

Dylan wasn't sure he wanted to admit the connection with Lucy. Especially with Otis there. "He's from camp. His sister and mom had an emergency, so I'm letting him tag along until they're back."

Alyssa gave him an approving smile. "Good on you. Let me know if you need anything."

She went back up front, pausing to give them a thumbs-up when the *ting!* of a hit rang against the walls. Dylan turned to find Otis staring at the bat like it was a magic wand.

"Told you she knew what she was talking about," Dylan said. "Now, let's work on stance."

"Okay!" Otis posted up at the plate eagerly, ready to learn.

A warm feeling stole through Dylan's chest. It wasn't every day he was part of blowing a nine-year-old's mind.

But now things with Lucy were more complicated. If he was honest with himself, there was a pull there, even if he wanted to cling to his "no girls" rule to maintain his focus on the future. He had a plan, and Lucy was a monkey wrench. She made him feel…alive. The pull was even enough to obliterate some of the heartache over Alyssa. But what would Otis think? This kid needed someone, badly.

Watching Otis light up as they worked on his batting,

Dylan made his decision. No matter what he wanted, Otis deserved more. He'd stay friendly with Lucy, but for her brother's sake, he'd leave it there.

And if Dylan was kind of frustrated by that, so what? Better him than Otis.

Chapter Fourteen

Lucy

"We'll keep her here for another hour or two," Dr. Westfield was saying. "Give the medicine a chance to fight back. She needs to be kept quiet for the next few days, though."

Lucy focused on the picture on his desk. A pretty, petite girl in a Texas A&M sweatshirt stood smiling in front of some college building.

"My daughter," he said. "She'll start her sophomore year at A&M in the fall."

The obvious pride in his voice made Lucy's heart ache. Her dad had sounded that way when she won a design contest or made A's. *When* she made A's. But still…that "dad warmth" tone was a sound she missed so much. "That's exciting."

"It is. But, back to what I was saying… Lucy, it's very important that your mother takes it easy. Stress seems to be a big trigger for her worst episodes."

His forehead was wrinkled. No doubt he was looking at Lucy and wondering how a girl younger than his daughter would manage all that. She wondered the same thing. Her to-do list was longer than I-35 at this point. "Okay. I'll watch the shop for her and make her stay off her feet."

"Good." He paused. "I know it's hard, having your father gone. You're doing a remarkable job juggling everything. I just wanted you to know that."

The tips of Lucy's ears burned. She didn't *feel* like she was doing a remarkable job. Her brother was stranded after camp and not answering her texts, the shop was idling closed on a busy Wednesday, and she was having a hard time standing up straight under the pressure. "Thanks."

"If you need anything, we're here." He stood. "If you're hungry, the nurses always have snacks hidden in their desks."

She nodded and slipped out of his office. Mom would be okay, but he was right. How often had Lucy seen Mom rubbing her forehead this summer? Lots. She'd just have to do better at helping out. Maybe take on fewer new projects or spend less time at Serena's with the chickens.

And she definitely didn't have time for boys. Which shouldn't be hard, since Dylan had been a complete ass that morning. She could brush him off and focus on her family. Like Dad would want.

So why was she so disappointed?

Before she went back to Mom's room, she tried Otis again, this time resorting to a phone call.

"Hello?" an older, deeper male voice answered.

Panic spiked through Lucy, sending a flush up her chest. Low and angry, she asked, "Who is this?"

"Whoa, there, tiger." The guy laughed. "Otis, there's a crazy lady on the phone for you."

"Hi, Lucy!" Otis's voice was bright and excited. "How's Mom?"

Lucy's jaw worked. He had no idea how worried she'd been. And he'd assumed the "crazy lady" on the phone was his sister. He wasn't wrong, but that kid… "She'll be fine, but where *are* you? And why is some…some *man* answering your phone?"

"Man?" Otis cracked up. "It's Coach Dylan. He took me to lunch, and now we're at the batting cages and it's awesome! This girl, Alyssa, totally knows about bats, and I'm going to need a new one. We had onion rings for lunch, and Dylan even let me have a shake. I got chocolate, because it's good, and I ate —"

"Slow down, Otis. Let me get a word in, huh?" Lucy's shoulders dropped from around her ears. Dylan was taking care of her brother. That was a surprise. Or was it? He wasn't the type to leave a camper hanging, but the idea of him entertaining a nine-year-old kind of bent her perception of him a little. "Put Dylan on, okay?"

"Hey." Dylan sounded a little out of breath, and there was a smile in his voice, like the whole thing had him amused. "I should've had him check his phone sooner. Sorry he missed all your texts."

"Sounds like he was having too much fun to remember." Lucy leaned against the wall. "Um, thanks…for taking care of Otis. This is probably his dream come true."

"We're having a good time. Take care of your mom, and I'll keep him busy until then."

"It should only be a few more hours." She paused, biting her lip, wondering what she was about to get herself into, but somehow unable to stop. "I don't know how to thank you for this. Really."

There was an even longer pause on his end. "You don't have to do that. And…I'm sorry about this morning. I had a bad start, too. I shouldn't have taken it out on you."

Lucy leaned her head back and closed her eyes. "That's okay. I get it. But I'd still like to do something. I know how to make cakes. You have a favorite flavor?"

"Uh…" Dylan covered the phone and called something to Otis before coming back. "I, um, appreciate it, but I don't need anything. I was glad to help. Can we leave it at that?"

Lucy felt like she'd been slapped in the face with cold lake water. "Okay, seriously. Is it me? Because it's just a cake. I'm not offering to have your first born."

"Who are you talking to?" Mom asked, through the partially open door. "And that better be a joke, because I'm *way* too young to be a grandma."

Lucy waved her off, wanting to stay angry. That, at least, she understood. Dylan still hadn't answered, pissing her off more. "Yeah, it's me. My bad for not taking the hint."

"No…it's not that. I don't want to put you to any trouble." Dylan sounded uncomfortable. "We both have a lot going on. You need to focus on your mom and shouldn't waste time on me."

Lucy deflated. What was he saying? That seeing her was a waste of *his* time? Or that he didn't feel like he was worth *her* time? She wasn't sure which was worse. "Fine, okay, I get it. Tell Otis I'll call when we're on our way home, so you can meet us."

"Sure." Was it just her, or did Dylan sound frustrated? Was Otis giving him a hard time? Or was having to deal with her really that bad?

Well, whatever it was, she needed to take his advice and focus on Mom. "And tell Otis to be good."

She hung up without waiting to hear his response and rubbed a hand over her tired eyes. She shouldn't let Dylan get under her skin. He wasn't her type, not even remotely, so why did his brush off bug her so much?

Maybe because she had the feeling he was interested, but something was holding him back. Had he decided she was too weird?

He wouldn't be the first guy who did.

Lucy heaved a sigh and went to her mother's bedside. "Hey. How's the head?"

"Much better. My eyelid isn't twitching anymore, either." Mom gave her a tired smile. "I'm so lucky to have a quick-thinking girl like you."

Lucy smoothed her mom's hair back off her forehead, feeling a little of the burden shift off her shoulders. "I try."

"You do. Your dad will be very proud of you when he hears you took care of things...of me." Mom reached for Lucy's hand and kissed it. "Thank you."

Tears stung the back of Lucy's eyes. "You're welcome."

"How about Otis?" Mom frowned. "Who's taking care of him? Serena?"

"Serena's off with her dad looking at a new flock of pullets." Lucy chuckled softly. What seventeen-year-old girl knew what a pullet was...in this century at least? "Otis is with his coach. He's a nice guy. Apparently, he stuffed Otis full of hamburgers and ice cream, then took him to the batting cages. I told him we'd text on our way back."

"Coach Dylan?" Mom quirked a little smile, then winced a bit. "The one Otis was throwing a fit over earlier?"

"One and the same." Lucy went back to the visitor's chair and flopped into it. "Otis doesn't have to worry. Dylan isn't interested in me."

"Wait...was he the one you offered to bake a cake for? Are *you* interested in *him*?" Mom's eyes lit up. "Come on, you can tell me."

Lucy shrugged. "Maybe. I don't know. He's kind of... structured."

"Ah." Mom laughed, then winced again. "Okay, no laughing. Anyway, you might be outside his comfort zone, is that it?"

"I guess." That was a pretty good way of putting it, actually. "And he's too comfortable for me, if that makes sense."

"A little solidity in your life wouldn't kill you, you know." Mom waved a hand at Lucy's sharp look. "I know, not my business. I want both my kids to be happy. That's all."

Lucy picked at her fingernails. "I know. I don't really have time for any drama, though. Boys are way down on the priority list at the moment, including overly structured pitchers."

Mom's smile was a little sad, but she didn't press. "So… what's going on with the chickens these days?"

Lucy was relieved at the obvious subject change. "Serena's dad went to the town council meeting to protest the ordinance. They vote next week, so he'll have one more try to persuade them. But…oh, Mom…if they pass it, Serena's farm has to move outside town lines, and they can't afford it. They might have to sell the chickens to a less ethical farm."

"I'm sure the council will see reason. They don't have any close neighbors. Even if it's to keep people like us, who live in subdivisions, from having livestock, surely they'll give Serena's family an exception. Don't you think?"

"I doubt it."

They sat in semi-glum silence until the nurse came back to release her mother. Mom could walk on her own but was unsteady, so Lucy took her straight home, rather than to the shop like her mother wanted.

Lucy forced a confident smile. "Don't worry— I've got it under control. I'll reopen in the morning. I can drop Otis off early, teach your class, leave the quilt ladies in charge while I pick up Otis, and it'll all be fine." *And fit in all my other projects around the edges.*

Mom's face still creased with worry, like she'd read Lucy's mind. "I'll be okay to teach tomorrow. You have that wedding dress to finish."

"I'll stay up late and work on it." Lucy made her voice firm, hiding how tired she was and how much she chafed at being so contained. Her mother's health had to come first. If she worked too much too soon, the next episode might land her in the ER or in the hospital overnight. "Mom, Dr. Westfield said to rest. Come back Friday." She flashed a wheedling smile. "And let me have all day off on Saturday. Otis doesn't have camp, and I need a day of doing whatever."

"Deal."

Lucy texted Otis, then Dylan, to let them know they were coming home. And hopefully start a do-over on this day.

Chapter Fifteen

DYLAN

"Aww, I'm having a good time, though," Otis said. He dragged his feet as they walked through the Swing Away parking lot, scattering the gravel and raising tiny puffs of dust. "Can we stay out a little bit longer?"

Dylan rubbed his face. Was this what having kids would be like? If so, he didn't need to give that a try for a long, *long* time. "Your sister and mom are on their way, and I'm sure Lucy needs your help at home."

Lucy. Just saying her name made him want to kick himself. She'd offered to do something nice for him, and he'd turned her down. Not because he wanted to, but right when she asked, he'd caught Otis staring at him. Between that and the nutrition plan his coach had suggested last month, he didn't feel like he should take Lucy up on the offer for a cake.

But still. Seeing her after that was going to be awkward. He should've just said yes, and shared the cake with the team. Why did he always think of the right answer *after* he said the wrong thing? It's like he was doomed to act like a complete dork around this girl, no matter what he did.

And why the hell was it even bothering him? It wasn't like they were going to get together.

Grimacing, he climbed into his car, checked Otis's seatbelt, then started out of the parking lot, before stopping at the entrance. "Wait. Where do you even live?"

Otis gave him the address but didn't know how to tell Dylan the directions—thank God for GPS—and away they went. Dylan couldn't help thinking Lucy was putting a lot more faith in him that he would've in her, had the situation been reversed. Did that mean anything? Or was he reading too much into it?

They drove through town to a quiet, older suburb near historic downtown. The houses here were smaller than out by the lake. Older, too, but well kept. Lucy lived in a one-story surrounded by giant trees. The front shutters and door could use a new coat of paint, but otherwise it was more normal than Dylan expected.

He choked back a laugh. If he were honest, he kind of assumed Lucy lived in a tree house.

Otis eyed him suspiciously when Dylan hopped out to walk him to the door. "I'm big enough to go in by myself, you know."

"I know." Dylan pressed his lips together. "I want to make sure everything's okay, that you guys don't need anything."

He wasn't sure, but he thought Otis muttered, "And to see Lucy," as he marched ahead on their sidewalk. Cicadas sang overhead but not a branch stirred in the dead calm of a humid summer afternoon. The house had a quiet, lived-in look that twisted something in Dylan's middle. He used to think his house was that way, but now he saw it for what it was: impeccably decorated, with only a few rooms that were actually used. Had it always been so boring?

Dylan followed after Otis, who had his chin jutted out stubbornly and his thin arms crossed over his chest. "Do you have a key?"

Otis patted his pockets. "No."

Dylan, resisting the urge to ask why not, reached over Otis's head and gave the front door a few soft knocks. Lucy must've been waiting just inside, because the door flew open. "Otis! Thank goodness." She gave him a quick hug. "Mom's resting, so don't tear around, okay?"

"Whatever," he grumbled, slipping inside. "Bye, Coach Dylan."

"Hey!" Lucy caught his arm. "Do you have anything else to say to Dylan?"

Otis heaved the kind of sigh only tween boys with older sisters could muster. "Thanks, Coach Dylan. I had a good time."

Then, with a somewhat wounded look, he disappeared around a corner and out of sight. Lucy watched after him, frowning. "Did something happen?"

Dylan shook his head. "He's probably just tired." *Maybe she'll believe that...*

"Crashing from the carb-load lunch." She gave him a wry smile. "Sure you won't let me repay you somehow?"

"It wasn't a big deal." Dylan scuffed a foot along the worn brick porch, not meeting her eyes. "He's a good kid. I'm glad I could help."

"I am, too." She reached out to touch his arm and he looked up, just in time for her to swoop in and kiss his cheek. "I was determined to say thank you, you know."

A flush burned up the back of his neck. "That was a good thank you."

She laughed, blushing. "I, um, better go back in. Mom's better, but she's pretty dizzy, and I don't want her to get up on her own."

"Yeah, good idea. I'll...I'll see you tomorrow." Dylan gave her an awkward little wave. "Bye."

"Bye."

The door closed as he walked down the sidewalk. He couldn't help looking over his shoulder. Lucy was obviously tired, with dark circles under her eyes and her pink hair limp. Very different from the mischievous girl at the lake. Had she even eaten today?

Guilt ate his gut like it had monster fangs. It sucked being caught in the middle like this, and one member of the Foster family would end up hurt, no matter what he did. Telling himself that Lucy was stronger, older, and would want Otis to be happy didn't help. Sticking to his pledge not to get involved didn't, either.

Because being involved sounded...good.

Shaking his head, Dylan started his car and pulled away from the curb.

For the next few days, Otis rode with another camper. Dylan caught himself looking up every time Otis arrived to see if Lucy was with him and had to deal with a pang of frustration whenever she wasn't.

On Friday, Dylan couldn't stand it anymore. "Otis, where's Lucy?"

Otis shrugged. "Running the store. She's busy, so I rode with Max."

Busy. *Or is she avoiding me?* Dylan could believe that more readily. She struck him as independent, and relying on another family to drive Otis didn't seem her style unless she had no other choice. "Yeah, okay. Go run your laps. I'll see you back here in a second."

Otis dropped his bag and took off. He was still the

fastest pitcher on the field. And he was developing a nice little fastball. He was already more accurate than the others, making it to the catcher's glove more often than not. Dylan couldn't actually let them throw more than 10-12 pitches a day, to keep the kids from injury, but Otis soaked up every word of instruction and had learned to apply it.

This kid might end up *better* than Dylan was.

The boys came running back. One, a pushy little punk named Jacob, shouted—*shouted*, like Dylan was deaf, "When are you gonna teach us curveballs."

Dylan crossed his arms over his chest. "When you're thirteen, and only if you can control a fastball, an off-speed, and a changeup."

Jacob stamped his foot. "But *my* coach says we can start *now*."

Dylan clenched his fists. Jacob's coach was an idiot. "No curves."

Jacob opened his mouth again, but Otis stepped in front of him. "Coach Dylan is a good pitcher. He knows what to do. So shut up and listen."

The boys squared off like two young bucks about to butt heads. Dylan put a hand on each of their chests and pushed them apart. "Thanks, Otis, but I'll take care of this." He turned to Jacob, ignoring the kid's scowl. "I won't teach you curves because I don't want to be responsible for injuring one of you guys. I *throw* curves, but I didn't in games until I was in high school, and that was on purpose. Any good pitcher practices one thing, and one thing only, until they've mastered it— throwing hard and making the ball go exactly where you want it. Do that, and you'll strike out more batters than most. Now, on the grass for stretches."

He blew out a breath and paced away from the group for a second. Good thing it was Friday. He needed a break from these guys, and they needed a break from him. Besides, Uncle

Rick would be there tonight, and he needed to focus on his own goals for a while.

Tristan, who'd sent his boys to sprint drills—and was grinning like an evil mastermind while they ran—strolled over. "Having some trouble?"

"Naw, just a kid who wants to have elbow surgery when he's twelve." Dylan paused. "You free for lunch today?"

"Sure."

"Good."

"You okay?" Tristan peered him. "You're…kind of spaced out today."

"I'll tell you more at lunch. I need to go wrangle my pitchers."

Maybe Tristan could help him navigate the quicksand that was Lucy Foster. And even if he couldn't, having another opinion wouldn't hurt. Dylan needed to do something, but he had no idea what.

The rest of camp dragged. It was the first time he hadn't loved every minute, and he resented the fact that his mind was so divided. Why was he letting all this bother him? And why—*why?*—couldn't he stay on track with his No Girls policy? Bit by bit, he'd felt his focus slip ever since they hit the playoffs last year, at the worst possible time.

But then he'd think about Lucy, dancing in the rain with her head thrown back, her hair stuck to her neck in damp coils, her shirt clinging to…everything. When that memory hit the queue, he was powerless to *stop* thinking about her.

It irked him. For Otis's sake, for The Plan, surely he could shove off thoughts of a girl he barely knew. A girl who was, in fact, the exact opposite of Dylan. Someone bound to drive him absolutely crazy, and not in a good way.

By the time the last boy waved good-bye, Dylan wished he hadn't asked Tristan to lunch. What he really wanted was to cannonball straight into his pool, not even waiting to change clothes, then climb out and fall asleep in his hammock. The sun scorched the field, turning the infield dirt into a desert and raising shimmering heat waves on the asphalt in the parking lot.

Dylan put away the last of the equipment, including a few things the boys inevitably left behind, locked the closet, and hit the showers. Tristan was already changing, so he knew he had to hurry, but standing under the barely warm water, just for a minute, felt like heaven.

"Dude, I'm starving!" Tristan called.

Groaning, Dylan turned off the shower and wrapped a towel around his waist.

He rounded the corner into the locker room, planning some retort...

And ran into—*literally ran into*—Lucy.

Chapter Sixteen

Oh my Gods and Stardust. Lucy's brain went tilt and rebooted. "Uh, I…oh, shit."

Dylan was…wearing nothing but a towel and dripping wet. And his face… If she weren't so flustered, this would be hilarious. His expression was frozen in shock, his cheeks fiery red.

But he was *half-naked*. No, he was *naked*-naked, except for the towel. Yeah, she was never going to be able to form a coherent word again. Flat stomach, good pecs, strong shoulders…what was *under* the towel?

A choked laugh from someone else shook her loose from her full-blown meltdown. Tristan, Dylan's friend from the lake, stood from where he'd been sitting on a bench. "Lucy? You know this is the men's locker room, right?"

She took a hurried step away from Dylan. "Yeah…sorry. The coach said you guys kept the kids' lost and found in here, and I just…Jesus. I'm leaving."

She turned and marched back through the door on shaking legs. As soon as the door swung shut behind her, though, she burst out laughing and slid down the wall to sit with her face in her hands.

She wasn't the only one. Tristan was practically dying on the other side of the door. "Christ, man, your face. Your *face!*"

"Shut up." Dylan sounded embarrassed, but Lucy could hear that he was on the verge of laughing, too.

Good. He'd been really stiff around her…wait, bad analogy. She started laughing again, and called, "I'm really sorry! I think I went in the wrong door."

Tristan poked his head out of the locker room, wearing a huge grin. "No, you didn't. We have an equipment closet in here. I think our coach probably imagined you'd knock first."

Lucy groaned. "I'm an idiot."

And she didn't regret it one bit. She'd gotten an eyeful, and she wasn't sorry *at all.* "Once Dylan is done hiding, he'll be out." Tristan came to sit next to her. "We were just going to lunch. Want to come along?"

She sighed, kind of wishing she could say yes. "I'd love that, but I'm supposed to be working. I'm only here because my brother left his glove behind, and I closed the store to run up because he was freaking out that he'd lost it forever."

Tristan laughed. "I can see that. Otis is really into playing ball."

"Yeah."

"My girlfriend met him a few days ago. Her dad owns the batting cages on Route 27. He made an impression— She thought he was adorable."

"That's a typical reaction. He's a good kid." Lucy smiled. It was so nice to hear Otis was in his element with these guys. He needed more of this. "But thanks for saying it."

The locker room door creaked open. Dylan, hair still damp, but wearing shorts and a T-shirt, peeked outside. He held up a glove. "I think this is Otis's. It has Foster written on the webbing."

"Oh, good." She stood and took it, and her fingers brushed his. A swooping sensation tugged at her stomach, and she met his eyes. His cheeks were pink but he didn't look away. She swayed slightly in his direction. Stupid, but she couldn't help it. "I think he was hoping I'd talk you into delivering it in person. He won't stop talking about 'Coach Dylan this' and 'Coach Dylan that.' He's got some serious hero worship going on."

"Aw, man," Tristan said, pouting. "I want kids to worship me."

The suddenly guarded look on Dylan's face stole some of the humor. "Yeah, about that…"

Tristan stood abruptly. "Oh, look at the time. I'm sure there's somewhere else I need to be. Like Snaps."

He strode off without a backward glance, and Lucy chuckled. "He's funny."

"He can be." Dylan squirmed, and Lucy knew for sure something was wrong. "Look, I…I don't even know how to say this."

She cocked her head, wondering if this was the part where he told her to leave him alone for good. Somehow, though, she couldn't convince herself it was. "Just say it. I'm a no-filters kind of girl, and I appreciate that in other people."

At that, Dylan took a slow step toward her. "Okay. I like you. A lot. I want you to know that, because I think I hurt your feelings when I turned down cake."

Lucy felt different shades of hot and cold, all over. "Then…why did you?"

He reached out to run his fingers along Otis's glove until they brushed hers again. "Otis told me he didn't want us to go out."

"I see." And she did. That was the hell of it. Her brother needed a father figure — or at least an older brother type — so badly that sharing was probably out of the question, at least for Otis. The fact that Dylan understood that only made her like him more, though. He seemed to get it.

A chill stalked down Lucy's spine as she realized what they were about to do. Funny, she didn't need this boy in her life right now. But…she wanted him to be, right when things went from a little weird to way too complicated. "Our dad, he's out of the country."

"He told me. I know what it's like to be a younger brother. And I know what it's like wanting something so badly it hurts." He glanced away. "Which is why I think we can't let this go any further. Whatever 'this' is."

Her heart ached, heavy and dull in her chest. A year ago she might've been able to tell herself *at least I saw him in a towel* and leave it at that, but she'd changed as much as Otis had, and she needed something, too. It wasn't fair, but Otis had to come first. She and Dylan both recognized that.

And all the other things on her plate had to come second. Which sucked, because she could really use something new. To dip her toe into the pool of excitement that came with discovering there was a person who could make her pulse jump with a look.

She nodded, her movements feeling stiff and jerky. "You're right. Thanks for telling me."

Dylan reached out, paused, then put a hand on her arm. "I wish things were different. I really do."

She nodded, feeling nothing but tired. This wasn't how things should be, but they were. "Me, too."

He stared at her a moment, opened his mouth like he was going to say good-bye, but changed direction at the last second. He stepped in close and, with a sigh, pressed his lips to hers.

It caught Lucy totally by surprise, but she leaned into him all the same. His shirt was damp, and she could feel the warmth of his skin through the cotton. He smelled like generic shampoo from the guys' aisle at Target, but it worked on him, and her knees shook. His arm slid around her waist, pulled her closer, pressing her against his chest. His lips moved slowly, gently, against hers, almost like he was memorizing how she felt in his arms.

Why did something this good have to be so confusing?

Knowing this could only get harder every second they clung together, Lucy let go first. Dylan's expression was…she didn't even know. Defeated? Resigned? Frustrated?

Because she felt every last one of those things, too.

He pressed his forehead to hers, sighed, then pulled away. "See you around."

"Yeah, see you."

She turned and walked blindly to her dad's Jeep, feeling gut punched. She'd had a tendency to date guys who were either a little pretentious or a lot wild, and breaking up had hurt, but not too bad, like her heart had never been all that tangled up in it.

So why did it hurt this much to walk away from a guy light years beyond her type?

"Girl, Otis needs to learn he doesn't always get his way. Hey! Stop it, Sprinkles. My boot is not food." Serena nudged the hen away gently before dropping a few extra treats in front of Sprinkles.

"Uh huh, says the girl spoiling her misbehaving hen." Lucy scattered more grain across the pen's floor watching the hens' wagging rears as they rushed toward the food. "It's just…it's not like that. Otis has needed someone like Dylan in his life since Dad left, and I'm a big girl. You have to make sacrifices for kids."

Serena stared at her, mouth open. "Lu, you know I love Otis, but he's your brother, not your son."

Serena was an only child. She probably didn't understand. "Being a big sister means you're 'second-Mom,' really. Especially since I'm eight years older. Hell, I changed that kid's diapers. I gave him bottles, sitting on the sofa, propped up with pillows. When my dad was called up when he was five, I taught Otis to ride a bike. I'm *responsible* for him. And Dylan seems to feel the same way."

"I think that's the first time I've heard the word 'rcsponsiblc' lcave your mouth."

Lucy dusted off her gloves, pretending that it didn't matter. "I have a lot of work to do, and with Mom being sick so much, I've had to help out at home and the store. Otis is a good enough excuse to keep from letting anything happen with Dylan. I don't really have time for a guy, anyway."

"I think the key word in that sentence is 'excuse.'" Serena shook her head. "We need to get up to some trouble, shake off this newfound maturity."

"I *am* off tomorrow. Mom's well enough for the half-day, and if I work on the wedding dress all morning, I can free up the afternoon. What do you want to do?"

"Egg Town Hall."

Lucy laughed and held up an egg from her basket. "And waste your beautiful, organic, free-range eggs? You get six dollars a dozen for these. Don't waste them."

Serena motioned her out of the pen, then closed the gate behind them before starting for the next chicken run. "Dad presented at the council meeting. It didn't seem to do any good."

Serena's tone had gone from outrage to outright sadness. "What aren't you telling me?"

"If the vote goes against us, we'll have to sell the flock.

Lucy sucked in a breath. "I thought you had a sanctuary lined up for them."

"It's too expensive to move them. They'd have to be certified by the vet that they don't have bird flu, and... basically, it would cost eight thousand bucks to move them, but there are commercial farms in east Texas willing to buy them and pick them up." Serena drooped against the fence. "Dad *says* they're good farms, but how could they be as good to Sprinkles and the others as I am?"

Lucy's chest felt tight as she reached out to hug Serena. "They couldn't. You're right. We need to do something, but what?"

"Something to make a statement, since Dad wasn't able to get through to them." Serena stood up straight, her eyes gleaming with anger. "Something public. That'll call attention to it."

Lucy was nodding. "When's the vote?"

"Next Thursday night. Dad's going to the meeting to make a last-ditch plea."

A smile spread across Lucy's face. "I have an idea. We'll probably get in big trouble, but they won't be able to ignore us."

Serena's expression was iron. "What do you have in mind, oh, devious bestie of mine?"

"A sit-in outside the Town Hall building." Lucy rubbed her hands together. God, she loved plotting. "Hen style."

Serena gave her a high five. "What do you need?"

"Some large crates and some hay. And some poster board." Lucy paused. "You know we'll probably get tickets for disturbing the peace, right?"

"I don't give a damn." Serena turned toward the pen. "Right, Sprinkles? We give zero fucks about tickets."

"It's settled then."

They exchanged evil grins and went back to feeding the hens and collecting eggs. Their plan was going to almost make up for the situation with Dylan.

Almost.

Chapter Seventeen

DYLAN

Tristan was still laughing. Hell, he'd probably be laughing for the entire school year. And maybe it was funny, but Dylan was too raw to care. That kiss…it'd been amazing, how Lucy fit against him. But the kiss was also like a good-bye, and they hadn't even really had time to say hello yet.

He'd had enough and gave Tristan a kick under the table. "Stop already."

Tristan pretended to wipe a tear from his eye. "God, that was hilarious." He made a face—eyes wide, mouth open. "I wish I had a picture of your expression."

Dylan had a sudden thought that left a sick feeling in his gut. "Please tell me you didn't set Lucy up to walk in on me."

"No, I'm not that sneaky." Tristan gobbled down a french fry. "I guess Coach didn't think we'd have plans and might want to shower before we left. And why would he?"

Right—why would he? Most of the time they limped out to their cars and drove straight home, sweaty and dust covered.

Tristan's favorite server at Snaps would've disapproved of that, so they'd cleaned up first.

Dylan dropped his forehead to rest on the table. "That's it. I have to move to another state."

Tristan threw a napkin at him. "Dude, we flaunted every chest on the varsity team last year. You hit three homers, shirtless, in front of, like, eight hundred people. Why are you so freaked out now?"

That was enough to make Dylan raise his head. "Because Lucy probably didn't go to the fundraiser, and because I wasn't shirtless, asshat. I was naked!"

"And she *really* looked." Tristan shifted in his seat to avoid the napkin sailing back his way. "I'm just saying she's definitely interested. What are you going to do about it?"

"Nothing." Dylan stirred the ice in his tea glass with his straw, wishing Tristan would just drop it. "It's a non-starter."

"What? Why?" Tristan pointed at him. "If you tell me it's your no girls rule, so help me — "

"It's not that, although I can't help thinking I'm dodging a bullet." At Tristan's raised eyebrow, Dylan held up his hands. "It's Otis."

After he explained everything, including his field trip with the kid, Tristan leaned against the back of the booth. "Wow, man. That sucks."

"It does, but we're both okay with it, I think. Otis is Lucy's first priority." Dylan took a bite of his hamburger. It tasted like cardboard. A shame, since Snaps had the best burgers in town. "And the minors is mine. Not taking it any further is probably the best for both of us."

"I wasn't commiserating because I agreed with you, dude," Tristan said. "I think you two might be fun together. She'd definitely blast some crazy into your life, and you need that. Isn't there some way you can talk to Otis" — he laughed — "man to man maybe? I remember being that age and Keller told me he wanted to have a man-to-man talk about something…it wasn't even important, but I felt like a big shot."

A little spark of hope lit in Dylan's chest, but quickly faded. "I can't do that to Otis. I can't put that on him, force him to choose. It's a no-win situation for him."

Tristan looked thoughtful. "You ever considered majoring in education and coaching youth baseball, like middle-schoolers? Because you've got the heart for it."

"Can't major in anything if I'm not going to college." Dylan stared Tristan down, daring him to say something. He didn't. "Maybe I'll coach U14 someday. After I retire."

"That's a long way off, no matter how you get there." Tristan drank a big gulp of soda. He didn't have to worry about sugar affecting performance, or where he was going after graduation. Oklahoma State had thrown a scholarship at his feet, and Alyssa liked the idea of going to Stillwater, so they'd banked on that. Together.

A future, all planned. Dylan's gut twisted with envy. He had an *idea* of his future, but a lot of it was out of his control. He had the grades to get into almost any college he wanted, and UT, Texas Tech, and Baylor had all offered him scholarships to come play. But that wasn't what he wanted.

Maybe Uncle Rick could help him, give him pointers on how to forge his own path into the farm system.

He refocused and found Tristan watching him sadly. "You know, there's more to life than baseball."

Maybe for him, but not for Dylan. "But it's the only thing that matters."

If only it could be that simple.

Uncle Rick's tricked-out Dodge Ram was parked at the curb

in front of the house when Dylan made it home. Smiling, he parked in the driveway and hurried inside. "Hello?"

Uncle Rick came into the entry from the living room. He wasn't a big guy—only five-nine and medium build—and people had a hard time seeing him for the outstanding shortstop he'd been for fourteen years in the majors. Retiring to his ranch had weathered him some, too. He looked like a cowboy now, right down to the scuffed boots and sandblasted Wranglers. "There's my favorite pitcher!"

"That's because you can hit everything I have." Dylan accepted Rick's firm clap on the back. "You look like saddle leather, Uncle Rick."

"I've been rounding up cattle for the last three weeks." Rick showed him calluses on his hands. "As far as retirement gigs go, ranching isn't a bad deal at all."

"What happened to your hands?"

"We had to rope some calves. One was a strong little bugger—dragged me a dozen feet before stopping. I had on gloves, so think what would've happened if I hadn't."

"Being a cowboy sounds more dangerous than I thought." Dylan followed him into the living room. "Where's Mom?"

"She ran to the store. She's making that chicken dish I like so much for dinner and needed some things." Rick collapsed into Dad's favorite chair. "She said Jack will be home around six."

"Yeah, he's been working a lot. But…I'm glad they aren't here. I wanted to talk to you."

Rick rested his elbows on his knees and leaned forward. "I figured. What's up?"

"Mom and Dad are pushing college. They don't understand why I'd want to go straight into the minors. They think I need a 'fallback' plan or something. How can I convince them otherwise?"

"You can't." Rick settled back in the chair. "Your dad

watched me struggle my way up after high school, but that was different. I wasn't all that great in school. Your dad was—and so are you. What's so terrible about college?"

Not him, too. "I have a plan."

"Hmm."

Dylan rolled his eyes. "What *hmmm*?"

Rick's expression hardened. "Plans are destroyed the second you sign a contract. The club owns you, pure and simple. You don't control your destiny outside of what you produce on the field. You can't network or study your way up the chain— A huge part of it is luck. Right place, right time. Can you roll with that?"

Dylan mashed down the panic rising in his chest. "I can. If I can just get into the farm system, I know it'll all be fine."

"Let me give you a stat…only ten percent of minor-leaguers ever make the majors. That's ten percent of the guys good enough to move into professional play. Only one percent of high school players make it straight to farm on top of that. A year or two of college won't kill you—or your chances—at all. What it might give you is another passion outside the game that will sustain you if a fickle career doesn't work out."

Doubt chased its tail in Dylan's mind. He knew he had the stuff. He *knew* it. All he needed was a shot and to work very, very hard. "I can always go back to college later."

"Without the scholarship, and with some wear and tear on your body." Uncle Rick rubbed a hand over his face. "I'm sorry. I'm not trying to dissuade you. I want you to have all the facts, is all. I won't lie to you and say the hard work wasn't it worth it— It was for me. If this is absolutely what you want, I know some scouts in the area. I could put in a call for a quick looksee this summer, give you some idea of where you stand before you rule out college ball before commit day. Okay?"

That seemed fair. "Okay."

He could do this. He could prove to them he was ready

to play pro ball. And if part of him wondered how lonely he'd be, and where Lucy planned to go after graduation, well… that was sheer weakness. He wasn't going to be benched by weakness. Not today, not ever.

Chapter Eighteen

LUCY

Lucy woke up late on Saturday, momentarily confused. She and Serena had plotted and planned late into Friday night, painting poster board, locating a few large empty crates and filling them with straw, and skulking around Town Hall at midnight to scope out the best place for a sit-in. She'd finally felt like herself again, up to something in the name of her favorite cause. She'd been so hemmed in the last few days, it was nice to plan a little mayhem.

Mom had been waiting up when she slipped in around twelve-thirty. The eyebrow arch conveyed a pretty strong message: *You're late. Again.*

Lucy had smiled and said, "Sorry. Serena and I got carried away with some work for the chickens."

Mom had looked at the mud-caked rubber boots in Lucy's hand and relented with a sigh. "Remember curfew is midnight. I don't like sitting up worrying about you."

"Okay."

She'd gone to her room meekly, knowing that her mother would have much more reason to be angry next Thursday night. Better to be contrite now, when she'd likely come home with a ticket in a few days. All for a worthy cause, but a ticket just the same.

Plus, what kind of brat daughter kept her recently sick mother waiting up for her?

Guilt stirred in Lucy's gut, even as she lay in bed with the summer sun streaming in her window. She should've thought of that. Should've come home by, or before, curfew to check on everyone. But after all that mess with Dylan, she hadn't wanted to slip back into her role as "responsible young adult." Now, though, she had to.

Lucy struggled to sit up and stretched. The wedding dress was folded on her desk, ready to be worked on. Sighing, she went to shower and grab a bite of toast.

She had a good-size worktable taking up almost the whole wall under the window. Between the sun and the strong swivel lamp mounted on the corner, this was the best place to see when doing delicate work. The house was quiet—Mom always took Otis to the store on Saturday mornings—and for an hour, it was peaceful to sew in a sunny corner, with only the swishing of tree branches outside for a soundtrack. But being alone, in a quiet house, gave her too much time to think.

Never a good idea, that…because thinking led to thinking about boys which led to thinking about Dylan which she really shouldn't do.

And why not?

Lucy growled inwardly at that tiny voice in her head. She didn't have much of an answer, except for the work and the sound of Otis's voice when he was out with Dylan. He hadn't sounded that full of joy or excitement in months. How might it hurt her brother if she pursued something with Dylan, and would that outweigh the maybe-ness of a good thing?

What about when camp was over? It was only two weeks, and they were halfway through. What would—*could*—Otis say then? Would Dylan still be in his life, or would she be in the clear to test the waters without betrayed and disapproving glances from Otis?

By then, she'd be over the hump with a lot of her projects, and she'd planned to take on less work during the back half of the summer, anyway, to have a little fun before school started. That had always been the plan—even before Dylan dropped into her life.

And if she was going to follow that train of thought to its full conclusion…why was she keeping her distance now?

Yeah, thinking never went the good and proper direction where Lucy was concerned, and she knew it. But watching Dylan let go of some of his armor that day in the rain, just for a minute, had been the most amazing thing. She knew they'd rub against each other's nerves like sandpaper sometimes, but maybe that's what they both needed.

Plus, those abs…and those arms? Seeing him yesterday, all flustered and damp from the shower? Yeah, she would never be able to erase that from her mind, which only made her want to see him more, to decide if a spark really was there, or if her reaction to him was some weird hormonal thing from being thrown together when things weren't going well. The kiss told her something was there, but she couldn't be sure without seeing Dylan again.

She glanced at the wedding dress. Another hour. She'd work on it for another hour, then text him. She probably shouldn't—but she had to know. Once and for all. If it wasn't going to work, she could put Dylan out of her mind for good.

Motivated, she hunched over the dress, her needle flying. With the end goal in mind, her rose vine design was on point, and she finished an entire foot along the hem in fifty-five minutes—a record. Distracting boys must be the answer to getting shit done.

Feeling like she was good to take a short break, Lucy picked up her phone, chewing her lip. Dylan had been kind of clear about not seeing her again. What could she say or do to convince him to meet her somewhere? What would interest him enough to say yes?

Wait…that's it…

L: *Thanks again for hanging out with Otis. Question… if I wanted to learn to catch a baseball for him, who could I talk to? I want it to be a surprise.*

Okay, there. Hopefully he wouldn't send her to the team's catcher, or a coach.

Little dots popped up under her message. He was texting back. She folded her hands, prayer like. *Please say yes. Please say yes.*

D: *You really want to learn? I didn't think baseball was your thing.*

Of course it wasn't her thing, but that was the point, right? *It's for Otis.*

And for her, but she'd leave it at this for now.

It took him a while to reply. *Okay. Meet me at the little league fields in an hour.*

Lucy's pulse took a flying leap. He was going to meet her. If there were fireworks during something as simple as catching lessons, she'd know. If there weren't, she could move on.

She finished off another inch on the dress, then changed into the lone pair of running shorts she owned, along with a gray T-shirt with a chicken saying "Moo!" on the front. She really did have too many T-shirts with chickens on them. This was probably better than the mash up T of Winnie the Pooh dressed as Chewbacca, though. She wasn't sure where the line was when it came to straight-laced Dylan. He might laugh. He might not.

She frowned, staring into her closet. So what if he laughed? If he didn't like Chewbacca-the-Pooh, he probably wasn't worth chasing. Fine, she'd wear her knee socks with the robots, tacos, and rainbows on them, too.

Shirt changed, she ran downstairs to grab a granola bar on her way out. Mom and Otis always went to lunch after the shop closed, a standing date for them to have some one-on-one time. Lucy had a few hours left to meet Dylan and be back home before they wondered where she'd gone.

The day was breezy and bright. Lucy's T-shirt stuck to her back before she made it to the car and a full AC blast didn't dispel much of the heat. Summers in Texas weren't for the dainty, that was for sure.

She drove through town, avoiding Main, where Mom's shop was. No sense in raising any drama if she could help it, right? She'd driven to the little league fields a billion times with Otis, and there were plenty of ways to get there that didn't involve cruising right by the store's front door...or getting lost. Besides, a little covert driving would take her mind off seeing Dylan. Butterflies were already holding a square dance in her stomach, and she wasn't sure she could handle much more.

When she pulled into the small lot, only one other car was there: a charcoal Porsche crossover. The tailgate was up, and Dylan was leaning into the back, his face hidden from hers.

"Okay," she breathed. "You can do this."

Being nervous was so stupid. She was never nervous before meeting up with a guy. Excited maybe, but not palms-slick, knees-trembling, stomach-fluttering nervous.

But she was.

She made her way through the gate and onto the field. A catcher's mitt, a chest guard, and a helmet with a mask were lying on the ground by the metal thing that kept pitches from hitting the spectators.

Just how seriously was he taking this? "Is all this stuff for me?"

The tailgate slammed closed. "Yeah, just a sec."

Dylan, carrying a basket of baseballs with a glove resting on top, came striding in from the parking lot. He was dressed in his usual: Tight, dry-fit T-shirt and athletic shorts. When had she started thinking that was sexy? Maybe it was the way he moved in those clothes—confident and sure. Like nothing could touch him. Like he owned the ground he walked on, but was willing to share it with her.

Heat crept up her neck that nothing to do with the brutal sunshine.

He carried the basket to the pitcher's mound, then turned to face her. "Overkill?"

She looked down at the catcher's equipment, hoping he hadn't caught her gawking. "Maybe a little. I was thinking more about tossing a ball back and forth."

Dylan cocked his head. "Not for Otis. There are nets and things that will let him pitch on his own, but if you really want to catch for him, you'll want to do it the right way."

Lucy held in a sigh. He was in full instructor mode. She'd have to work around that if she wanted to crack his resolve. And she *really* wanted to try. "Maybe show me how to hold a baseball the right way, and we can work up from there?"

His eyes narrowed. "Otis could teach you that."

"I want *you* to teach me."

That hung in the air between them. Dylan looked away, but his shoulders were tense. Good, someone knew how she felt, too. "Lucy…"

She wasn't going to hear any excuses. Serena was right— She needed to cut the crap. She marched over to the bucket of baseballs and pulled one out. She walked over to Dylan, stopping a foot away, and held up the ball. "Show me."

His head snapped up. The heat in his gaze burned straight through her, and she had to bite back a smile of triumph. She had his attention now. And someone liked girls who took control.

A line knit between his eyebrows, and his shoulders were up around his ears, but he didn't tear his eyes away from hers. "Okay, I'll teach you, if that's what you want."

His voice was soft, not annoyed, as he moved around to stand behind her. His breath was warm on her neck and goose bumps raced down both her arms. His hands covered hers, helping her turn the ball, so it was in the right spot against her palm, before moving her fingers into the correct position.

Lucy hardly breathed.

"This is how you hold the ball—always hold it across the seams." He gripped her hand in his larger one, and mimed throwing the ball, not like a pitch, but like one of the other players would. "This is how outfielders throw, but it's all you need to send the ball back to Otis."

He mimed the throw again, moving her arm overhead. "You'll release it from the top. Think you've got it?"

Lucy wanted to say no, just so he'd keep holding her arm, but she nodded. "Let me try."

He stepped back, and she took a deep breath. Her hands were shaking. *You can do this. Maybe.* She regripped the ball like he'd shown her, wound up, and threw.

The ball went about ten feet, bounced off the ground, and rolled.

Dylan couldn't stifle his chuckle. "That was…uh, that was good for a first try."

Lucy put her hands on her hips. "It was terrible. Let me try again."

He dug three balls out of the basket and handed her one. She threw the first one farther, but way to the left. Grumbling, she held out her hand for another ball. This time, she managed to throw it mostly straight.

"You know?" Dylan still sounded amused. "This might be good for Otis. He'll have to practice fielding balls that come off the bat on a hop anyway."

"Is that a nice way of making lemonade out of my lemon of an arm?" Lucy asked.

Dylan winked at her and trotted into the field after the balls. Lucy watched as he bent to pick them up. She had to admit, the view was pretty spectacular.

She didn't quit ogling him in time, and Dylan straightened up to find her staring at him, twirling a piece of hair around her finger. He strolled over, grinning. "What?"

She smiled back. "How do I catch a pitch?"

"You'll have to put on the mask and guards, first."

Lucy went for the gear and put it on. "Now what?"

"You squat."

His voice was daring her to do it. Fine. She dropped into a crouch and punched the mitt a few times. "Like this?"

"Uh, yeah."

His voice had cracked—now she was getting somewhere. She waggled a bit, crouching deeper, and grinned when he watched her, slack jawed. "Show me what you've got."

A fresh smirk. "I throw pretty hard."

What, did he think she was made of glass? "Prove it."

Mumbling something she couldn't hear, Dylan paced around the mound a minute, then settled down to wind up. The pitch that came at her moved much faster than she expected. She caught it, barely, then pulled her hand out of the mitt and shook it. "Ow. You win."

"Hey, you caught it. That's something." He was nodding in approval. "That's good for the first time."

"You're a good coach. I see why Otis likes you so much." She stood, stretching the kinks out of her back. "Speaking of which, I need to be honest. I wasn't here just to learn to throw a ball. Truth is, I wanted to see you. I couldn't think of a way to convince you unless Otis was involved somehow."

Dylan took a few steps off the pitcher's mound, inching closer. "I guess that's fair."

She took a more obvious step toward him and pulled off the helmet and chest plate. "I appreciate you worrying about Otis. I do. But…he's old enough to understand, and I want to get to know you."

"We're totally different." Dylan's voice grew rough. "Opposites—"

"*Opposites* sometime attract." Lucy took another big step, closing the distance to about ten feet. "That's part of the fun. I'm not saying I want a proposal or anything. Just coffee."

"We already had coffee." To her surprise, he came three steps closer. His fists clenched, unclenched. "Maybe…"

She waited, watching an obvious war play out via the expression on his face. He wanted to try this thing out as much as she did, but his so-called "better nature" was holding him back. Feeling bold, she closed the distance, standing right in front of him. "Maybe, what?"

He took in a sharp breath, eyes fixed on hers. Dylan's eyes weren't as blue as she'd originally thought, but a stormy blue-gray. Intense and distant, kind of like how he could be sometimes. She hoped she could fix the "distant" part.

Finally, he reached for her hand. "How about lunch?"

Smiling, she gave his fingers a little squeeze. "Thought you'd never ask."

Chapter Nineteen

DYLAN

What am I doing? What am I doing? Dylan watched Lucy, long-legged and sure, as she strode over to pick up the catcher's equipment he'd brought along. He'd set it out hoping it would create a buffer, a "this is all business" gesture.

It hadn't worked. He should've known it wouldn't. This would probably end up way more complicated than he liked, but there was a definite pull between them. He'd thought if you gave a pair of magnets enough distance they wouldn't call to each other. In this case, he'd been dead wrong. Just watching her bend to pick up the catcher's helmet made his pulse race. She moved with catlike grace. She knew what she wanted and she went for it.

That, he could respect.

The fact that *he* was what Lucy wanted? As much as he hated himself for ignoring Otis, and for swerving away from his rule about no girls, knowing how much Lucy wanted to be here flattered him. It was exciting.

And damn hot.

Most of the girls he'd dated before were....well, proper was an old-fashioned word, but maybe traditional was more accurate. They weren't shy about letting him know they were interested, but they wanted him to take the lead, dropping hints until he asked them out. They wanted the full production—having him pay the check, waiting for him to kiss them, elaborate prom-posals, the whole deal. Fortunately, he was good at figuring out how to navigate the unspoken rules. Lucy threw the rulebook out, and it kept him on his toes.

He'd never kissed girls he barcly knew—or burned for the chance to do it again—until now.

Lucy glanced over her shoulder at him, her smile teasing. "Are we going to meet wherever we're going, or should I leave my car here?"

It was a challenge. The first of many, he supposed. "I'll drive."

Her smile widened— He'd passed the first test.

She helped him carry everything back to his car, then hopped into the passenger seat without waiting to see if he'd open the door for her. Yeah, definitely not traditional.

"Where are we going?" she asked. Her cheeks were flushed, but he didn't think it was the heat. "I'm not dressed for anything too fancy."

"Dolly's?"

She nodded. "I owe you a burger, so that's good."

They didn't talk much on the way to the drive-in. After all her brash behavior, Lucy seemed to have gone shy on him.

He liked that, too.

Once they parked and ordered, he decided he had to say something. "So, um, you're a senior next year, right? Where are you going after high school?"

"Design school, with a minor in business. I like to do needlepoint, but I sew, too. My mom taught me young, and I want to turn it into a career like she has. Texas Women's has a good program and it's local. With my dad in the Army, I get a break on the tuition, too. You?"

He hadn't expected her to have such a concrete plan. He blinked. "Um, baseball. I'm going to try to get into the minor league farm system."

"Farm system?" Lucy's nose wrinkled. "When I think of that, I think of Serena's chickens, not baseball."

He gave her a blank look. "Serena has chickens?"

Suddenly conversation was a lot easier. Lucy's chicken T-shirt collection made more sense, too, although he had to admit the Pooh/*Star Wars* mashup was funny. "Where do you get all those shirts?" He reached out and fingered the hem of her sleeve. "They're hilarious."

She flushed. "You don't think they're stupid?"

"No. Just because I'm boring and wear Nike and Under Armor all the time doesn't mean I don't like fun stuff."

She bit her lip, eyes shining. "You know, the first time I met you, I thought you had a stick up your ass."

He laughed outright. "My friends tell me that all the time. I like to think I'm focused, but maybe I'm just uptight. I don't mean to be. I just have a goal, and I'm willing to do anything to make it happen."

"I can respect that. Uptight isn't the same as disciplined, so I'll cut you some slack." Lucy put her shake in the cup holder and reached out slowly to rest her hand on his knee. His entire nervous system centered around the touch of her fingers on his skin. "You ever watch *The Breakfast Club*?"

He wasn't sure he could form a sentence with her hand on his leg, but he managed. "My mom made my sister and me watch it a few years ago. Said it proved she knew what it was like to be a teenager."

"Remember when the weirdo and the jock got together?" Her lips curved in a mischievous smile. "This could be kind of like that."

Dylan cleared his throat, glad the A/C was blasting. Otherwise he might have melted by this point. "You aren't a weirdo."

"Oh," she whispered, leaning closer. "You really have no idea."

His pulse stuttered. No, he didn't…but he wanted to. "Try me."

He cupped a hand around the back of her neck and brushed her lips with his. Her hand tightened on his knee, and she deepened the kiss, teasing his lower lip with her tongue. His temperature shot up another thousand degrees, and he might never, ever catch his breath again, but he couldn't focus on anything but the feel of her mouth against his.

Then, there was a knock at the window.

"Damn it," he breathed. With a sigh, he turned.

Nate, their shortstop, grinned and waved, motioning for Dylan to roll down his window.

He did, giving Nate an annoyed glare. "Yes?"

"Oh, just thought I'd say hi!" Nate leaned to the side to wave at Lucy. "Hey!"

She laughed. "Howdy. So, you picked *right now* to say hi?"

"My timing is excellent." Nate winked at her and Dylan wondered if the shortstop would be able to play one-handed, because he was seriously considering rolling the window up on the one resting on the door. "How are things going?"

Dylan groaned under his breath, but Lucy, still smiling, said, "They *were* going really well. But I can definitely appreciate a solid interrupt." She held out a hand for a high-five. "Good work, my friend."

Nate turned to Dylan. "Okay, dude, I like her. I'll be on my way."

He waved and walked toward a car full of Dylan's teammates, who were all clutching their stomachs and laughing their assess off. "Asshats."

"I think they're funny. They respect you."

Dylan rolled up the window and raised an eyebrow at Lucy. "How do you figure that?"

"It's like kids interrupting their parents when they kiss or hug." She nodded in the direction of group of laughing guys. "They just wanted you to know you have their attention."

Sure, but he wasn't looking for attention. No, in fact he had an overwhelming urge to be alone…with Lucy. "Want to drive back out to the fields? No one's there."

Lucy sat up in her seat, hands folded in her lap. "I don't know…sitting in a car alone with a boy in a remote location? What will everyone say?"

Dylan's eyebrow twitched. "You said that with a straight face, even."

"I thought you might like girls who are worried about their reputations."

"You don't have to worry about me. At least, not about that."

She leaned back, giving him a look that burned him straight through. "What if I want you to surprise me?"

That was enough. He backed out as fast as he could without rear-ending anyone and drove back to the little league field. Lucy watched him, alert and curious as a cat. That's kind of what the whole thing felt like—like when one of his mom's cats gave him the time of day, but he felt like he was being examined for character flaws. How did those damn furballs do that?

He pulled in next to her Jeep and put the car in park, suddenly not so sure he was doing the right thing. There was a lot in the way of this working out, and he wasn't a "just have fun for a day or two, then part ways" kind of guy. Wasn't that why he'd sworn off girls? Because he had to go all in?

"Two-dollar bill for your thoughts." Lucy smiled, but

there were worry lines around her eyes. She was, he noted, also keeping her hands folded in her lap.

"My thoughts aren't worth two bucks." He scrubbed a hand through his hair, trying to keep his eyes focused on the steering wheel and not straying to Lucy's long, bare legs. It didn't work. "Look, I'm…this is a weird time in my life. I'm not sure I'm in a good place for a relationship."

She cocked her head. Her hair was coming out of its ponytail and a pink-tinged strand fell into her face. "What are you afraid of, really? I keep asking if it's me, and you keep saying no, but I'm kind of getting a complex."

He frowned. "Afraid? I'm not afraid."

Lucy put a hand on the door handle. "Yes, you are. I don't know what you're scared of, but you're scared all the same." She shook her head. "Call me if you decide I'm worth the risk."

Dylan felt her words like a punch to the gut, swift and painful. God, she was right. The word *risk* held everything he was worried about. *You're only seventeen, dumbass… How come you're acting like you're forty, and every decision has a life-ending impact?* Maybe he had goals. Did that mean he shouldn't try to live a little, too? Because it seemed like a waste of time not to.

And he hated wasting time. Especially when this girl made him feel alive and bright as a star.

Dylan caught Lucy's arm before she climbed out of the car. "You're right. I'm scared…but I don't want to be."

She let go of the door handle. "What *do* you want?"

"A chance to know you." He breathed out the words, hardly believing he said it. "A chance. That's all."

She settled back in her seat, searching his face. "You sure? I don't really like having my feelings hurt."

"I'll be careful with them. Promise." He held out a hand. "Hi, I'm Dylan Dennings. I like chocolate ice cream, going to the lake, and Westerns."

A slow smile lit up her face. "Westerns?"

"My dad and I used to watch them on weekends. Clint Eastwood is a badass." He motioned at his outstretched hand. "Your turn."

She took his hand. "Hi, I'm Lucy Foster. I like embroidering crazy stuff, pizza in all incarnations, and chickens."

He shook her hand then let it go, smiling back. "We kind of jumped into the kissing part of 'getting to know you.' Maybe we should've started here. Then I could've asked about the chickens first thing. What else do you like to do for fun?"

For the next hour, they talked. That was it. In the car for a while, walking on the trail until they were too hot, then back in the car. By that point, he knew the names of Lucy's favorite hens, had seen pictures of the goth wedding dress—amazing, really amazing—and found out her favorite color wasn't pink, but maroon.

"It doesn't work well on dark hair," she said, gathering a handful of her ponytail to show off the pink tips. "A lighter, brighter color pops more, so I did this instead."

He reached out, not even thinking, and ran his fingers through it. Her hair was silky soft against his rough skin. "I like it."

She closed her eyes and leaned into his hands. "I like what you're doing."

His heart banged against his rib cage. He was falling fast, despite what he said about taking time to get to know her. Completely sucked in, head spinning like the vortex of a tornado.

His hands shook a little when he reached back out, moving slow, to pull the ponytail elastic from her hair, letting it spill down her shoulders. He toyed with a strand, then dug his fingers into it at the back of her head, massaging her scalp and neck.

"You can keep doing that all you want," she murmured, her eyes still closed.

Dylan laughed softly. "My secret weapon."

"It's a good one." Her eyes fluttered open. They weren't quite focused as she cupped his cheek and pulled him closer. "I already know you're a good kisser, but I'd like to try it again…to make sure I'm right."

He shifted closer to her in his seat, until their faces were an inch apart. Her breath was warm on his jaw. "I'll do my best. This *is* for science after all."

Her eyes fell shut, and he leaned in…

Her phone buzzed, loud, from the cup holder. She jumped and pulled back. "Sorry about that." She looked at the screen. "Um, I have to go. My mom is looking for me."

The way she said it sounded like she might be in trouble. He couldn't understand why, but he nodded. "I had a good time."

Her smile was shy. "Me, too. We should do this again."

"Tomorrow," he said, thinking fast. He wasn't ready to let her go. "Meet me at the marina at three."

Before he could blink, she leaned across the seat and quickly brushed her lips against his. "Tomorrow."

He watched her drive away, knowing he was past any hope. Lucy had him, hook, line, and sinker.

Chapter Twenty

LUCY

Lucy cursed under her breath as she drove. She'd nearly lost her mind when Dylan started massaging her head, and all she wanted to do was spend the whole afternoon kissing away the worry lines around his eyes. Worry lines he probably didn't even realize were there.

But the text from Mom, while short on words had been full of meaning: *Why aren't you home?*

Before taking off, she texted, *I went to Braum's for milk.* Which now meant she had to buy milk on the way back. *It's crowded.*

M: *We have milk*

L: *Ice cream. I meant ice cream.*

Mom hadn't answered that one, and when Lucy walked into the kitchen with a bag full of sundaes and a gallon of milk, Mom was sitting at the kitchen table, waiting. Lucy had gotten The Stare. Her mother knew her well enough to never take a simple answer when a more complicated one was just as likely.

"Where were you really?" Mom asked, pausing when Otis ran in, yelling, "Ice cream? You're the best sister ever!"

Guilt stabbed through Lucy's gut. She should've been home working, or tackling the sink full of dishes her mom had obviously tried to start before tiring out. Her eyelid was twitching slightly, and the pinched lines of her face hinted at the beginnings of a migraine. Lucy put away the milk, resolving to start on the laundry and finish the dishes instead of seeing if Serena wanted help at the farm.

And if she felt stifled, it was her fault for seeing Dylan instead of staying home. She couldn't be sorry about it, even if she wished things could be different. What would she give for a quiet, lazy summer? Almost anything.

"Lucy? Are you going to answer me?" Mom asked.

Lucy waited until Otis took off with his sundae before sitting across from Mom at their old, wooden kitchen table. "If I tell you, will you keep it to yourself?"

Mom's eyes widened. "Should I be freaking out right now?"

Lucy shook her head and looked through the kitchen door to the living room. Otis must've gone to his room, because it was empty. "I met Dylan. For lunch. I didn't tell you because it came up suddenly and you were at the shop—"

"With Otis. I understand it now." Mom sighed. "Lucy, you don't have to feel guilty for liking that boy. He seems like a great kid."

"I know." Lucy ran a hand over a nick in the wood. She'd made that trying to cut her own pork chop when she was seven. She'd burst into tears for hurting the table. Dad had given her a hug and told her he was proud she'd tried it herself first before cutting her meat into tiny bites. "But it's hard. If I screw things up with his coach, Otis won't forgive me."

Her chest tightened. She missed her dad so much. His gravelly voice, his big presence, the way everything was always okay when Dad was around. He was her safety net— she saw that now—and she was having a hard time hanging on without him here to support her. But she had to. Mom and Otis needed her. She had obligations.

But what if she messed everything up? What if she disappointed him?

"We all want to shield Otis from distress, but we're not doing him any favors." Mom took a bite of ice cream. "I'll keep it quiet, though, until you and Dylan decide to tell him." She paused. "I'm making some assumptions, aren't I? That this is a thing and not just lunch?"

"It was just lunch, but I think it'll be a thing." Heat flooded Lucy's cheeks at the memory of his fingers in her hair. "He's different."

"I'd like to meet him for real some time, but I'm glad. You haven't had anyone in your life for a while." Mom smiled, and it erased some of the pain lines around her eyes. "I hope it works out for you."

"Me, too." Lucy got up to put her ice cream into the freezer. Now that the farce was over, she wouldn't have to choke it down after her lunch. "How are you feeling?"

"Better, but there's still a twinge or two. Thanks for taking care of everything." Mom stood and came to give Lucy a hug. "I talked to Dad this morning. He said to tell you he's proud of you."

A lump rose in Lucy's throat. "I wish I'd been there to talk to him."

"He's going to try to call again in a few days." Mom kissed the top of her head. "You probably have work to do. I'll let you get to it."

Lucy nodded and went to her room. Her knees still felt

a little shaky from her time with Dylan, but her hands were perfectly steady, and she settled in to work.

Sunday morning, after their usual pancake breakfast, with fresh eggs from Serena's farm, Lucy shot her mom a loaded glance. "I have plans this afternoon. I'm going to Serena's then out for a bit. I've finished the laundry, and I'm almost done with the wedding dress. Do you mind?"

Lucy had stayed up until one-thirty to work on the wedding dress and had only quit because her eyes kept crossing. She was close enough that she could finish it tonight and start on the other projects tomorrow. She'd also finished the laundry and the dishes, and with the shop closed today, she felt like she'd earned the break.

Otis looked up from his syrup-smeared plate. "Where?"

"Out with friends." Lucy hoped he'd drop it. "Nothing special."

Mom gave her a wry smile. "Fine with me. Home before ten, okay?"

Ten? Was she serious? Yeah, based on her expression, she was. Lucy nodded, knowing better than to argue about this one. "Before ten. Got it."

"Can I come? I haven't been to the farm in a long time. I can help," Otis said.

Lucy's heart constricted, and she forced herself to be logical—Otis *was* a big help, but she could take him some other time. She had every right to go out by herself without guilt. "Sorry, not today. Besides, you need to rest up for camp tomorrow."

Otis frowned, and Mom stepped in. "I have an idea. Why don't you invite a few friends over? I'll make brownies, and you guys can play on the trampoline, or ride your bikes."

Otis brightened immediately, and Lucy mouthed, *Thank you* over his head at her mom. Mom winked and went back to washing dishes. She seemed a lot better today. Good. One less thing to worry about.

Lucy went to her room and threw a hodgepodge of things into a bag: towel, rubber boots, a straw hat, sunglasses, and flip flops. At the last minute, she grabbed some sunscreen, too. No telling where she'd end up today, but she'd be prepared.

Lucy laughed. *Prepared*. Not a word she'd use for herself all that often. Must be Dylan rubbing off on her.

When she got out of the Jeep, Serena's dad was hooking a hose up to the spigot on the side of the house. He waved at her, pointing at the house. "We're filling up some kiddie pools for the hens. Serena's out spraying down the runs. There's some frozen squash in the cooler by the first pen. Mind handing those out?"

"On my way." Lucy tugged on her boots. After helping out for two years, she knew really hot days were bad for the hens. They'd get sick fast when overheated.

Serena's family had already erected shades over the runs to help cool things down, and the hens weren't frolicking like usual. Even the flock's rooster had a sluggish strut. Lucy dug out a dozen pieces of frozen squash and scattered them about. The hens were more enthused by that and started pecking at the cold cubes.

She made her way through two more pens before running into Serena, who was plugging a fan into an extension cord. She nodded at the cooler. "Guess you ran into Dad? We need to cool them off before we lose any."

Lucy didn't bother answering, instead hurrying off to finish handing out squash to the rest of the overheated chickens. By the time she circled back, the first flock was starting to show more signs of life. Serena handed her another cooler. "Frozen strawberry slush. They love it."

So Lucy made another round, dropping doughnut sized disks of strawberry ice into each pen. It took so much care to keep a flock like this going. It wasn't just to provide people with organic eggs— Serena's family truly loved what they did. Her mom was a physician's assistant, giving her dad the time and means to manage the farm. It was such a shame that the town was going to force them to sell the flock.

She didn't think the sit-in would change the council's mind about letting them stay, but that didn't mean they shouldn't try.

When she dropped the empty cooler up by the house, Lucy found Serena sitting in the shade of a giant oak, chugging a bottle of water. She flipped one to Lucy. "It's two-thirty. Didn't you have somewhere to be at three?"

Lucy glanced at her phone. Where had the time gone? "Yeah, but he'll understand if I need to stay here and help."

Serena raised an eyebrow. "There's a hot baseball player waiting for you at the lake, and you want to stay here with me and a bunch of chickens? Did you hit your head or something?"

"No...but if you need my help, I can stay."

Serena shook her head firmly. "We're good, now. Besides, my beloved is on his way over. If we need anything, he can help."

Lucy gave her a disbelieving look. "Didn't he trip over a rake and fall in a mud puddle last time?"

"Yeah...he's adorable, smart, and very sweet, but he doesn't know the first thing about working outside." Serena laughed. "Still, it's cute when he tries."

Lucy patted Serena on the leg and stood. "Okay, then. I'll go." She paused. "Do you think I'm the worst sister ever?"

"For going out with Dylan?" When Lucy nodded, Serena rolled her eyes. "No. You're a good sister for even worrying about it. But, seriously, forget about Otis for a while and enjoy this."

Enjoy it. Right. She could do that. "Okay. I will."

"Go change out of those nasty farm clothes in the shed before you go. And I want a full report tonight!" Serena called after her. "No skimping. All the details. You hear?"

Lucy gave her a thumbs-up and, after changing into her swim suit and a sundress as ordered, she climbed into the Jeep, wondering what Dylan had in store. A flutter started up in her stomach. Butterflies always sounded like a silly way to describe it. Zombie butterflies she could live with. Something with panache, and little weirdness. Moths, maybe.

Whatever it was, she couldn't squash the feeling. That's how she knew it was true: she was falling for a type-A athlete.

Whoever would've thought?

Chapter Twenty-One

When Dylan went downstairs to ask if he could borrow the Sea-Doo, he had no idea he was walking into an ambush. But that's what he did.

Abandon all hope, ye who enter the kitchen.

"Honey, Uncle Rick and I were talking," Mom said when Dylan came in looking for Dad. All three of them were at the table, nursing cups of coffee. "He knows the batting coach at Texas Tech and thought you might like an introduction."

Uncle Rick shot Dylan a look that was half-apology, half-determination. Dylan ground his teeth. "If I don't have any offers, maybe I can do a gap year. I can meet the coach then and start when I'm nineteen. What's one year off?"

His parents exchanged a weary glance, but Uncle Rick pounced on it. "Tell you what, if they aren't biting by October—because you'll know by then—then I can introduce you to Jerry."

Dylan could almost see the thought bubbles above his

parents' heads. *This could do it!*

He fought to stay calm. Yelling and storming out never worked—they'd dig in harder. "Fine, whatever. Dad, can I borrow the Sea-Doo? I have a date."

Dead silence. Mom was obviously fighting back a smile, though. He realized they'd been worried about *this*, too. Dad gave him a sly look. "I thought girls were off the menu this year."

The hope in his voice, the desperation—*maybe this is a sign!*—broke something inside Dylan. They didn't understand what drove him. They never had, and never would. Uncle Rick should've gotten it, but even he was on their side.

And Dylan was done. "You know what, forget it. I'll see if Tristan will let me borrow his boat."

He turned to leave, but Dad stopped him, sounding resigned, "You can borrow the Sea-Doo. Don't drive it after dark, okay?"

Dylan nodded without turning back. He wished they could see what he saw each time he picked up a baseball—a path, lighting up in front of him. Do step A, B, and C, and watch his dream come true. If for some reason he didn't make a team, he could find a part-time job, take community college classes, and work out with a coach. He didn't love the idea, but it was better than completely admitting defeat and heading off to Texas Tech, or wherever.

He went to the garage to hook the trailer up to his car. He was looking forward to this date, and he wanted it to be perfect. The last thing he needed to do was stew about his parents' lack of confidence in his pitching skills or his determination to make something happen. He wanted today to be about getting to know Lucy, for real. And if he was breaking a rule he'd given himself to do it...well, the temptation was too strong.

It wasn't that he had lost focus on The Plan. He just

couldn't resist seeing her again. Who knew, maybe Lucy would do for him what Alyssa did for Tristan. And even if she didn't, he was happier either way. That had to help, right?

His phone vibrated in his pocket while he was connecting the wires from the trailer to the hitch on the Porsche. Tristan, asking, *So, Nate told Ledecky who told me you were making out with Lucy at Dolly's yesterday.*

Dylan sat up, shaking his head. *Dude, that was the most convoluted text I've ever read.*

T: *So were you?*

D: *Was I what?*

T: *Don't be a d-bag. Were you with Lucy yesterday?*

D: *Yeah. And I'm taking her out on the lake today.*

T: *Good. I was worried you'd be all noble about her kid brother. You have that tendency.*

Dylan rolled his eyes. Tristan *didn't* have that tendency. *I'm less noble than you think.*

T: *Then go forth, my son, and have a very wicked afternoon.*

Dylan laughed. *Do my best.*

By the time he made it to the marina, he felt better. He could almost forget about the squeeze play at home, with Uncle Rick as the sacrifice bunter trying to help his folks run it in. He backed the trailer down the ramp until the Sea-Doo was in the lake and could float off the platform. Once it was set, Dylan climbed out to free the Sea-Doo from its cables.

"What'cha doing?"

He glanced up, squinting in the strong afternoon sun. Lucy stood at the edge of the ramp, dressed in an aquamarine bikini top, covered up by a white sundress that stopped at mid-thigh.

What *had* he been doing? "Uh…" Dylan blinked. *God, dumbass. Get ahold of yourself.* "I thought you'd like to go out on the lake. Give me a hand?"

She nodded and tossed her bag into the car, shed the dress—which pretty much fried Dylan's entire brain—and splashed into the water. She proved surprisingly adept at helping him remove the cables. "Want me to park the car? That way you can pull the Sea-Doo up to the dock?"

He stared up at her. Miles and miles of tanned skin glowed in the sun. Dylan swallowed and was dismayed when his voice cracked, "Yeah, that'd be great. I have a life jacket in the backseat for you."

With a funny little smile, Lucy hopped down and climbed into the Porsche. She revved the engine a bit, leaning out the driver's window, eyebrows raised. He shook his head, laughing, as she pulled out, sedate and careful.

Dylan breathed. When he'd said come to the lake, he'd had this in mind, but the sight of her in yet another bikini had his engine redlined. He shucked his shirt and shoved it into the saddlebag on the side of the Sea-Doo. He'd put bottled water and a couple of granola bars into the other side, and the tank was full, so they were set for a long afternoon.

Lucy strode over, carrying his keys and wearing the life jacket. He was a little sorry to see the bikini covered up, but safety first, right? Once his keys were stowed, he pulled the towrope so he was against the dock and held out a hand. "It's a little bumpy."

"Just how I like it," she said, sliding onto the seat behind him easily. "So, cowboy, show me how this thing handles."

Her arms came around his waist and she slid in close, her thighs brushing his. *Yeah, the Sea-Doo was the best idea ever.* "Hold on tight."

"I'm planning on it," she murmured in his ear and goose bumps spread down his arms.

Dylan started up the Sea-Doo and pulled carefully out of the marina. As soon as they passed the "no-wake" and last speed limit sign, he opened it up. With two people, the craft could still do almost fifty miles per hour, and hearing Lucy's squeal torn away by the wind was plenty of motivation to crank the throttle and send them hurtling across the top of the water.

There wasn't much of a breeze, which kept the lake still and allowed them to streak faster and faster. Dylan cut hard a few times, sending up waves of water, and grinned when Lucy hollered, "Again! Again!"

He'd taken girls out on the lake before, but almost all of them had come off the Sea-Doo with shaking legs and a request to ride around in Tristan's boat instead. It wasn't that the little craft was scary…or maybe it was with the way he drove it. He liked to push it hard, have the wind beat into his face, and jump wakes to catch a little air.

When they came close to the coast on the far side, Dylan cut the speed and glided into a little, crescent-shaped cove. It was too small and shallow for most boats, so it was deserted, just like he'd hoped. When they were in waist-deep water, he turned off the Sea-Doo, then slid off to pull it up onto a sand bar. Lucy slipped off after him and swam out a little bit before floating back to the shore.

"That was amazing!" Her eyes were glittering. "Please tell me I can drive it."

"Liked that, huh?" Dylan dropped to the sand right at the edge of the water and took off his life jacket. "Sure, I'll let you drive it."

Lucy came out of the water, dripping, and sat beside him, flinging back her damp hair. Seeing his jacket on the sand, she wriggled out of hers, too. "This is awesome."

Yeah, it was. He felt the knots in his shoulders unwinding. What was it about Lucy? Sure, she sometimes—*often*—drove him nuts. But she also cast some kind of spell over him. He reached out and tentatively brushed a strand of hair from her jaw. "I'm glad you said yes."

She looked up at him from beneath thick lashes. "I'm glad you asked."

Dylan took her hand, turning it over. "I was worried about getting sucked in. I have so much riding on the next year, I didn't think I could take the time to meet someone. Then you fell into my life and I can't keep away from you."

"I thought you were going to be this boring jock." She nudged him, one bare shoulder against another, and sparks danced down his spine. "And you keep surprising me."

"So…" He mustered up his courage to say what had been on his mind since yesterday. "Does this mean you'll give us a chance?"

"Only if you will." She flashed him a wry smile. "I get how important your sport is to you, your plans. I would never make you choose— I know what having a passion is like. But I don't want to be a convenience."

"You're anything but convenient, Lucy Foster." Dylan cupped her cheek in his hand. "And I like it that way."

She shifted closer on the sand, until their legs were touching. "So, you'll deal with my crazy?"

"Deal with?" He brushed a kiss against her cheek. "That's the part I like best."

Chapter Twenty-Two

Lucy

The part he likes best? Lucy laughed softly. "You may be the first guy to say that."

"I mean it. I need a little fun, and you showed up when I needed you most, I think. Kismet or fate or something." His face was so close. His *lips* were so close. Ready to be kissed. And she wanted to, all afternoon long.

"Maybe I'm actually some kind of mystical creature." She smiled. "I'm here to grant you three wishes, earthling."

His expression was mock-thoughtful. "Let's see. Number one, I want to be the ace pitcher for the Texas Rangers. Two, world peace."

She gave an airy wave of her hand. "Done. And three?"

"For the girl sitting on this beach to kiss me."

Thought you'd never ask. "Hmm, that takes a more hands-on approach, I think." She slid her arms around his neck. "Close your eyes and wish upon your favorite star."

His eyes fell closed, and she could almost see the wish

on his lips. Sighing softly, she leaned in. Her mouth met his gently, light, like the wish. His arms came around her waist, pulling her closer. They were both damp, with the sun hot on their backs, and pressed skin to skin. It was just a kiss, but it was so much more.

A wish come true? Maybe.

His hand tangled in her hair, and they fell back onto the sand, mouths never breaking apart. He was solid and warm against her, and she traced the muscles of his arms, his back. Yes, definitely some perks to dating an athlete. He bit her lower lip, just a nibble, and she shivered despite the sun-warmed sand at her back. Then his fingers slid down her arm, drifting to her hip. His touch sent shock waves through her middle. She had to give him credit—he knew what girls liked, and wasn't in it just for himself.

The kiss went on and on, until she finally had to pull away to catch her breath. "Wow."

He gave her a cocky smirk. "Just what I wanted to hear."

"I'll give you that one." She kissed his jaw. "Now, can I drive?"

Dylan laughed, and it lit up his face, turning the little lines around his eyes into sweet crinkles instead of worried creases. "Should I be worried?"

"My dad taught me to drive a stick shift, which I drive every day, thank you very much." She jerked her chin at the Sea-Doo. "How hard can it be?"

He raised an eyebrow. "Wait, that Jeep is a manual?"

She shrugged. "So?"

"You keep saying I'm full of surprises…Lucy, I don't know a single girl, and probably only three guys, who can drive a stick. It's impressive."

Funny thing, he really sounded impressed. Like driving a car was a big thing. "My dad is a lieutenant colonel in the Army. Do you really think he'd let me off so easy when it comes to driving?"

"When you put it like that…" Dylan stood and waded into the water. "Should I be worried he's going to hunt me down for kissing you?"

"Nah." She frowned. "Well, maybe."

"It was a pleasure knowing you, Lucy." Dylan made like he was going to get onto the Sea-Doo and leave her on the beach.

She laughed. "Honestly, he'll probably like you more than the other guys I dated." She smiled, remembering him scaring off a smug art student she'd met at camp one year. That boy had been a little too anarchic for Dad's taste. "You have a military haircut and great posture. If you can run a mile in eight minutes or less, he'll be all for it."

"I can run two miles in fifteen minutes. That should do it." Dylan winked. "You miss him a lot, don't you?"

Tears pricked the back of her eyes, out of nowhere. Maybe it was Dylan's matter-of-fact-but-tender tone…or maybe it was that she missed her dad just that much. "Yeah. I can't go half a day without hoping he's okay. I…I missed a phone call from him yesterday. It made me sad."

"I miss my sister like that sometimes. Not as much as you miss your dad," he hurried to add. "But she's out of the country, and I'd forgotten what it's like not to be even able to text her when I want to. She's seven hours ahead, so I always — stupidly — think about texting her in the afternoon here, and it's already late there."

Lucy put on her life jacket and picked her way over to the Sea-Doo. "It's hard. But I think about how great it'll be to see him again, and it gets me through. Mostly."

Dylan's hands encircled her waist. "Grab the handlebars when I push you up. I'll steady you until you're on."

Steady her…yeah, because her heart wasn't pounding and her legs weren't shaking. Still, Lucy managed to climb onto the bobbing craft. In an act that was part athleticism and part sheer awesomeness, Dylan bent his knees underwater, then launched himself out of the lake to land sidesaddle on the back part of the seat. The Sea-Doo swayed but didn't tip.

Lucy's eyes went wide. *Damn.* "That was impressive."

"Eh, I do it all the time." Dylan slid onto the seat behind her and wrapped his arms around her waist.

Leaning forward, he clipped the key to her jacket and walked her through starting the Sea-Doo. She found it hard to pay attention with his breath warm against her ear, but she got the gist. "You ready?"

He laughed. "Ready as I'll ever be. Take it easy coming out of the cove. It's a blind exit."

Obediently, she put the little craft into cruise mode and glided them out of the cove at a calm five miles per hour. Once they were clear, though, she opened it up, and then they were flying over the water. Dylan laughed as she whooped with excitement. "Hold on!"

Dylan's hands tightened on her waist and she leaned into a turn, sending them skidding, then back again. Lucy didn't think she'd felt this untethered in a long, long time. It was amazing...she'd needed this.

Dylan let her drive for almost an hour, until they were low on gas. "We should go back."

Even though she'd had to slow down a lot to drive them toward the beach near the dock, her pulse was still tripping like a live wire. It wasn't all the ride, either. Dylan's arms were strong and tan, and water droplets glinted against his skin every time she stole a glance at them around her middle. The problem with dating artistic, or anarchic, guys, she decided, was a definite lack of tanned, taut skin. They tended to see outside labor of any kind as blasé. She'd broken up with two guys for questioning why she helped at Serena's farm. The vegan had broken up with her, calling her a murderer for picking up the eggs the beloved hens laid. She didn't have the heart to tell him Serena's flock laid unfertilized eggs, because that would've led them into a philosophical argument. Instead, she wished him well and decided to be single. There'd been too many guys with too many "constraints" where her passions were concerned.

She wouldn't have to worry about that with Dylan. Maybe that's why she liked him so much. For all their "opposites attract" baggage, they were still alike enough in ways that counted. Enough so that things striving to keep them apart weren't being all that successful.

Dylan leaned forward, giving her a quick kiss behind the ear. Lucy felt *that* in every nerve. "Can you hang out here until I back the trailer in?"

She nodded, admiring the view as he slid off the Sea-Doo and waded onto the shore. A buzzing under the seat made her quirk an eyebrow. *What the hell?* She laughed when she realized it was Dylan's phone, hidden away in a compartment under the seat pad. Not even thinking, she pulled it out.

A text from someone named…Rick? *I have a scout lined up for Wednesday. He'll set up a time with your coach. I'm heading home. Hang in there.*

Lucy wasn't sure what that meant, but as soon as the Sea-Doo was back on its trailer, she handed him the phone through the open driver's window. "Sorry, I looked. Is that good news?"

Dylan stared at the screen like the phone was going to bite him in the face. "Uh, yeah. My uncle played in the majors, and he knows a lot of scouts in baseball. I guess this means I'll have my first real shot on Wednesday."

Lucy leaned into the window and planted a kiss on his cheek. "That's amazing. Good luck! I'm assuming this isn't something I should show up to, you know, to cheer you on."

"No, probably not." Dylan's brow was wrinkled. "I wasn't

expecting this. I thought my uncle was starting to side with my parents on the whole college thing."

Lucy still couldn't quite get her mind around the *college is horrible* idea, but she could see it was important to him. "Looks like he wasn't after all."

"Yeah."

Dylan went quiet. She'd been about to suggest they drop her car off at Mom's shop and go to Dolly's or the cute diner on Main her family loved, but she wasn't sure what was going through his head. "You okay? I thought you'd be happier."

"I'm okay." He flashed her a smile that looked pasted on. "I had a good time today."

Lucy searched his eyes, finding confusion, excitement, and a healthy dose of nerves. This news had thrown him over the moon. "Me, too."

He nodded. "Maybe we should call it an afternoon, though. I need to get ready for camp tomorrow."

She tried not to feel brushed off. "Yeah, I have some finishing touches to put on that wedding dress, and I want to check on Serena, see how the hens are doing."

He nodded. "I'll see you in the morning, then."

"Sure."

She leaned in to kiss his cheek, but he surprised her by turning at the last minute to give her a quick kiss on the mouth. "Right. See you tomorrow."

Lucy took a step back, not quite sure what to say. Instead, she waved as he drove away, pulling the Sea-Doo behind him. He must really be freaked out by the news because he hadn't even waited until she got into her car. Frowning, not sure if the pang in her chest was hurt or concern, she went back to her Jeep. Her phone was in the glove box, and Serena had texted.

S: *Hey.*

S: *Oh, yeah. You're on your date. Sorry.*

S: *It's just…we lost Sprinkles. She couldn't handle the heat.*

S: *The rest are okay.*

Tears filled Lucy's eyes, and she threw the car into reverse. Maybe Dylan didn't want—or need—her right now, but Serena did.

By the time she pulled up to Serena's farm, having thrown on a T-shirt and shorts over her bikini, Serena's mom was waiting at the gate. "They're out back, hon. She's pretty broken up. She loved that hen." Mrs. Blake sighed. "They're going to bury Sprinkles. None of us could bear…"

She didn't finish, but Lucy understood. Usually, Serena was pragmatic and stoic about her hens, understanding what their life cycle entailed. Those that passed laying age were usually humanely put down and turned into fried chicken. It might sound cruel to someone on the outside, but it always sounded kinder to Lucy, whose chicken came from the market, and was usually from a large farm that didn't care about its birds. Serena's family was religious, and they prayed over each and every chicken they ate.

But Sprinkles was different, special. Serena had raised her from the shell, bought from a nearby farm that bred laying hens. Sprinkles had been a *pet*, more than the other hens.

Lucy tugged on her boots and went in search of her friend. She found Serena and her dad in the small garden behind the house. Mr. Blake was leaning on a shovel underneath a giant magnolia, and Serena held a cardboard box. Her eyes were puffy and red. As soon as she saw Lucy, she started crying again.

Lucy put an arm around her friend's shoulders. "I'm sorry, Ser. Sprinkles was a sweet little girl."

Serena swiped at her eyes. "I know I'm being silly, but I feel like it's my fault. I should've noticed the heat sooner, or brought out more ice, or…anything."

"You did everything you could, precious," Mr. Blake said. "You and Lucy both. Texas summers are rough on these birds. Their new homes will be pleased to see how well we've taken care of them."

A stab of guilt hit Lucy right between the eyes. She'd spent her afternoon frolicking at the lake, kissing a cute boy, while her friend frantically tried to save their chickens. Given how weirdly her time with Dylan had ended, maybe she should've made an excuse and stayed here.

That wasn't true, exactly, and she knew it. Still, it made her angry. The Blakes loved their farm, loved their hens. They were a mile from the closest subdivision and acres from their nearest neighbors. How could the town do this them?

Boiling, Lucy said, "We'll fix it, Ser. We'll fix it."

Her dad gave Lucy an odd look, and Lucy met his gaze head on. This was one fight she wasn't backing down from. No freaking way.

Chapter Twenty-Three

Disjointed thoughts crashed around Dylan's head the whole way home. He hadn't meant to react like such an idiot to Uncle Rick's text. Two miles from the marina, some of the shock had worn off, and he realized he'd been kind of rude to Lucy.

While he waited at a stop light, he texted her. *Sorry I ran off like that. I'm a little blown away by the news. See you tomorrow?*

And Dylan *was* blown away. Uncle Rick had come through in a big way. This was it—his chance to prove he had what it takes. Now he just needed to be ready for the tryout. Extra sleep, watch his diet, be careful when demonstrating pitches to the campers to protect his arm...he needed to commit to all of it. He only had three days, so he needed to pack in as much preparation as he could.

So why was it that his mind kept drifting back to Lucy driving the Sea-Doo? Her hair had tickled his face, and her body had been warm against his as they cut their way through the water. And the feel of her mouth on his had been nothing short of heavenly. Especially her little, "wow" afterwards. That was the kind of reaction he liked to hear after kissing a girl. And even though she'd said it out loud, he'd been thinking it, too.

Dylan rolled to a stop at a light on Main and shook his head. Much as he wanted to relive every second of the afternoon, he needed to focus. Soft skin and sweet smiles had to wait.

His parents didn't have much to say when he came home. Dinner was tense, and each scrape of a fork or knife sounded like an avalanche. His mother kept the conversation fixed on the neighbors' redecorating, and Dad made noncommittal noises ever so often. Dylan ate as quickly as he could, looking longingly at the baked mac-n-cheese when he piled an extra helping of salad onto his plate.

"Honey, don't you want some mac-n-cheese?" Mom pointed at the casserole dish, still more than half full of cheesy, golden-crumb goodness. "I thought it was your favorite."

"It is." Finally, Dylan couldn't take the elephant in the room. It was tap dancing on the table for God's sake. "I'm watching what I eat the next few days, before the scout comes out to see me. I need protein and veggies for that."

Dad set his fork down. "While I'm glad Uncle Rick is taking such an interest in your career, you've been acting like we don't care about you. If you'd told us, 'hey, I'd like to eat clean the next week for my tryout,' your mother would've substituted the carbs for broccoli. Just because we want you to consider college doesn't mean we're don't care about what you want."

Okay, that stung. "Then don't push college. Let me have a gap year. I don't even know what I'd major in."

"Lots of freshmen don't," Mom said, reaching over to

squeeze his hand. "We only want the best for you and to keep your options open. You're in binary mode: it's baseball or nothing. We're trying to help you see the big picture. That's all. If the scout likes you, we'll travel to whatever team you end up on and watch you play, bursting with pride."

Dylan stared at his plate. "I didn't know."

"Well, maybe if you'd listen to what we said instead of trying to guess at what we meant, this would've been easier." Dad sighed. "You're a very smart kid, Dylan. Honor roll, top ten-percent, excellent prospects. You're good at math and science. Heck, you could teach math and coach baseball if you didn't want to leave the game. But your mother's right— if you do make it, we'll be there, all the way."

"Thanks." Dylan looked up at both his parents. His mom's eyes were shiny with tears. "And…maybe I'll fill out some applications. You know, just in case."

His dad's satisfied grunt spoke volumes. Mom smiled at them. "Well, Dylan, I guess this means Dad and I are going to eat *all* the brownies I baked this afternoon. Pity."

Dylan groaned. "Now you're playing dirty."

"Yeah, because I need to lose ten pounds, and I thought my ravenous teenage son would save me from those brownies." She stood. "You know where they are if you change your mind."

Dylan held up a forkful of salad, less enthusiastic about it now. "Thanks, I'm good."

Floored by his parents' not-quite one-eighty, he headed to his room after dinner. He'd need a good night's sleep— because tomorrow his plan for MLB domination would be kick-started.

"A real scout?" Nate asked. He'd herded most of his campers

over to the third baseline to run warm-ups and came over to say hi. "For real. Like a major league scout?"

The awe in Nate's tone made Dylan flush with pride. "For real. My uncle set it up for Wednesday afternoon."

"Gonna be hot then, man." Nate scratched his head, mussing his dark hair. "That scout will be sweating his ass off."

"Heat's good," Dylan said. "It'll keep my arm nice and warm. Plus, I need to prove I can play under harsh conditions. That'll do it."

"No doubt." Nate gave him a fist bump. "I better get over there before Ledecky starts bossing the kids around like he knows what he's doing."

Dylan waved him off. His pitchers had gathered at the mound and were horsing around. Otis had arrived early, while Dylan was in the locker room wrestling the pitching shield out of the closet. He felt bad for missing Lucy—he really did—but maybe it was good he hadn't seen her. He needed to keep his head on straight until Wednesday.

He trotted over to his campers. "Good morning, guys. Everyone warmed up?"

"Yes, Coach Dylan," they shouted in unison.

"All righty, then. Split off into teams for catching practice. No pitching—throw like you're trying to surprise a runner who's floated too far off first plate. Okay?"

They nodded and jostled to pick partners. Otis stood aside. Dylan frowned. "What's up?"

"We're an odd number," he said. He was wearing a bright blue Under Armor T-shirt and a very serious expression. "I want to catch with you."

Otis's huge, pleading eyes weren't something he could refuse, so Dylan went to pick up his glove. They found an empty space near the first base foul line and Dylan lobbed an easy ball Otis's way. He caught and raised an eyebrow. "You can try harder."

Dylan laughed. "Big talk, there. Show me what you've got, hot shot."

Otis threw, straight and reasonably hard, right at Dylan's glove. The kid was good. *Really* good. He'd seen it, but there was a maturity about Otis's play that wasn't there with the other kids. He needed a coach, a real one, to develop what could eventually be college, or minor league, skills.

Problem was, if Dylan suggested that, Otis would ask him about coaching. That might cause some complications if Dylan kept seeing Lucy. Still…this kid needed more than a two-week camp could teach him.

The rest of the day sped by. He put the campers through their paces, hitting, pitching, stretching. A few of the boys were already getting restless. They weren't serious about it, but most of the others were, and that made Dylan proud. If nothing else, he'd given them something to work on in the next season.

When dismissal time came, Lucy was one of the first people there. She stood just outside the fence, waving at Otis—and Dylan. He walked over while Otis picked up his gear. "How's your day been?"

"Good." She smiled. Her hair was back in a ponytail today, its pink tips fluttering in the wind. "I'm, um, I'm going to Serena's later. Think you might want to join us and meet some hot chicks?"

Dylan laughed. "What guy wouldn't?"

"Well, these might shit on your shoes." Lucy gripped the honeycombed openings of the chain link fence. "They aren't exactly house broken."

He reached up to wind his fingers through hers. Not easy with the fence in the way, but the forced distance was kind of hot, to be honest. "It sounds good, but I need to focus on my tryout Wednesday. Rain check?"

He didn't miss the flicker of disappointment in her eyes,

even though Lucy merely shrugged. "Sure. I'm busy Thursday, but maybe Friday." She frowned. "Maybe."

Okay, that expression is concerning. "Why 'maybe' for Friday? Camp will be over."

"Oh, nothing. But maybe we should get together Wednesday night. Just in case."

He didn't like the sound of that. "Are you sure it's nothing?"

"Hey! Why are you holding hands with my sister?"

Dylan let Lucy go like he'd been burned. And in a way, he had. He'd forgotten all about the risk. Now Otis was standing behind them, hands on his hips. Dylan shot Lucy a glance.

"Otis, we should go. We'll talk in the car," she said.

He shook his head, glaring. "You promised."

"No, I didn't." She sounded so much more patient than Dylan could've been. "Let's go, okay?"

Otis gave Dylan a long, dark look, then stomped through the gate. Lucy smiled sadly at Dylan over Otis's head, then turned to walk him to the car.

Tristan came over, carrying a plastic tub full of baseballs. "What was that all about?"

"Otis caught me holding hands with Lucy."

Tristan laughed. "That's one protective kid."

"Not in the way you think. I could be in for some trouble over the next few days, and that's not exactly what I need right now. But it's my fault." Dylan rubbed a hand over his eyes. "Can you stick around for a while? I need to get some practice in with a live hitter before Wednesday."

"Sure, let me put this stuff up."

After Tristan left, Dylan watched Lucy's Jeep pull out of the lot. He hoped she wasn't in for it with Otis. But she probably was.

Chapter Twenty-Four

Otis's bottom lip stuck out. When he was little, maybe three or four, Lucy would tug on it and he'd start laughing. Surefire way to end a pout. But this wasn't exactly a pout. This was an older boy who didn't think it was cool to cry when his feelings were hurt and was fighting them with rage instead.

"I want you to understand it's not something serious, and I'm not hanging out with Dylan to hurt you," Lucy said. "He's nice, cute, and makes me laugh. Me going out with him doesn't change the fact that he thinks a lot of you."

Nothing. Otis only shifted deeper into his seat.

Lucy blew out a breath. "Dylan is a person, not a thing. You can't claim ownership to a teenaged boy. He has a mind of his own."

Otis continued to glare at the dashboard.

"Fine. Be mad."

The rest of the ride to the shop was frosty and silent. As soon as Lucy parked, Otis bolted from the car, leaving all his gear except his phone behind. Lucy took a minute to rest her forehead on the steering wheel, trying to decide if the tangled knot in her chest was anger, guilt, or…what?

You like him.

Yeah, but Otis is having a really hard time right now.

Sure, but does dating Dylan change anything? He'll still hang with Otis. Maybe even more because he'll see Otis on a regular basis.

You know Dylan's leaving, right? If he gets drafted, he'll leave Suttonville the day after graduation.

So? It's not like I want to marry the guy. A few months of fun would be worth it. Right?

Or would it? Because what kind of sister ignores her little brother's pain?

Someone knocked on the driver's side window. "Lucy?"

She looked up. Mom stood outside the car, frowning sadly. Lucy pulled the keys from the ignition and climbed out of the car. "He told you?"

"No, but I can guess what happened. He noticed something between you and Dylan…is that right?"

"It's not like we were kissing. We were barely even holding hands, *through a fence.* Otis lost it. Mom, am I a terrible sister?"

Mom laughed softly and pulled her into a hug. Lucy always felt safe, cradled close to her mother, and it still worked, even now. "You are a very good sister. Otis's possessive streak isn't your problem. He needs to learn to share."

"Tell Otis that."

"I will." Mom pushed Lucy away gently and held her at arm's length. "If you like this boy, your brother will get over it. Stop holding back for his sake, okay? I love that little stinker, but you deserve good things, too."

"Okay." Lucy took a deep breath, letting the air clear her head. "I should probably text Dylan. Let him know not to worry. Could you ask Otis not to take it out on him? Dylan has a big tryout this week, and he doesn't need to deal with the drama."

"Will do." Mom brushed the loose hairs from her ponytail out of her face. "I saw the wedding dress when the bride came to pick it up. Gorgeous work, honey. I was wondering…after college would you like to be my partner? You practically are already, and I'd like the shop to continue when I retire."

Lucy's heart leapt. This had been her most secret wish. Not building up her own store, but taking over Mom's. "Are you serious?"

Mom's warm smile yes. "Of course. That is, if you want to work with me."

Tears filled Lucy's eyes. "Oh my God. Yes! I'd love that."

"Good. I want you to go to college first, but you can work here during the summers and on holidays." Mom looked ready to cry, too, when she squeezed Lucy's arm. "Let's go inside. I'm about to melt out here."

Lucy followed, feeling punch drunk. What a seesaw twenty-four hours. She liked it, though. What was life without a few whiplash turns?

That night, after she'd gone to Serena's to help with cooling the hens down again, Lucy lay on her bed. Dylan hadn't texted all day, but it's not like they texted on a regular basis. Still, she thought she should check in. Otis had refused to talk to her at dinner, despite several stern and pointed looks from Mom. Not even the surprise of three Rangers' tickets for Saturday night made him blink.

Dylan probably needed to be warned what he was in for.

Besides…she kind of missed him. If someone had told her a week ago she'd miss a Type-A, super-driven ball player, she would've snorted. She'd always wanted chaos and Technicolor. How weird that someone who lived by rules could make her pulse race. Even better—what if she rubbed off on him? How awesome would they be then?

Lucy picked up her phone and texted: *Hey. Sorry about Otis.*

A few minutes later, Dylan answered: *Is he totally pissed?*

L: *Yeah, but even my mom is like, "Get over it, kid!" He'll be fine. We just need to give him time.*

D: *Also, probably shouldn't get too close when he's around, at least for now. He might explode.*

Okay, that wasn't Lucy's idea of helping Otis get over it. *Totally. We shouldn't get horizontal when he's around. I think he can deal with a little hand-holding, though.*

Dylan sent her an emoji with googly-eyes. *Wait, does that mean you *want* to get horizontal?*

Lucy laughed, feeling her cheeks go hot. *Slow down, there, buddy. It's not off the table, but let's figure out what this is before we think about horizontal time.*

D: *And what is this?*

L: *I don't know, exactly. But I like it.*

D: *I like you.*

Lucy curled around her phone, biting her lip. If anyone came in, they'd see her grinning a goofy smile. How sappy. She couldn't help it, though. Seeing a guy who came out and said, "I like you," without any bullshit or flowery extras was a new experience. Dylan merely said what he meant—how rare.

L: *You're pretty likable, yourself. Look, I know*

you're busy this week, but do you want to get together tomorrow night? Just for a little while?

D: *I can't stay out very late, but I'd like that.*

L: *See you at the picnic table at the marina at eight, then.*

D: *I'll be there. Um, are we playing Truth or Dare again?*

L: *It's a surprise.*

After they signed off, Lucy dropped back onto her bed, tracing her fingers over her lower lip. No matter what they did, she was definitely planning on some kissing. Who knew—maybe a good luck kiss or twelve would even help Dylan with his tryout.

Someone knocked on her bedroom door. "Come in!"

Otis pushed the door open and stepped into her room. Lucy sat up. "What is it?"

"Mom told me I'm being unreasonable." He blinked. "That's her word for it, anyway. So, I guess it's okay if you date Dylan, but only if you promise not to hog him."

Lucy swallowed a laugh. Otis's expression was so serious, like this was a business negotiation. "Define 'hog him.'"

"Pretending I don't exist. Being too busy to hang out with me. Or not ever taking me places because you're with him." Otis stood up straighter, his narrow shoulders square. "Don't treat me like an annoying little brother."

Wait a minute…was he mad because she was going out with Dylan, or was it because she was going out with someone at all? Some of her past boyfriends hadn't been all that interested in being civil to Otis. She'd even broken up with one for calling him a brat.

Maybe Otis was upset about both things: that neither

Dylan, nor his sister, would have time for him anymore.

Lucy wrapped her arms around her stomach, feeling more than a little sick. "Oh, Otis…I'm sorry if that's what you think will happen. I know things have been busy lately, but it wasn't because I think you're annoying. I've just been trying to help out more. But, I promise I'll still have time for you if I have a boyfriend. I'm sure Dylan will, too."

"Good, because I want to ask him if he'll give me pitching lessons on the side. Is that okay?"

"Absolutely. I'll even help you pay him. I have some savings from my projects." Lucy held a hand up, like she was giving an oath. "Cross my heart."

Otis gave her a sharp, dignified nod. It was so adorable, Lucy had to hide a smile. "Thanks, but I have my birthday money from Grandma."

"Are we cool then?" Lucy asked.

"Yeah, I guess." Otis shrugged, his businesslike demeanor falling off in a blink. "But I still don't want to see you kiss him. That's gross."

"Give it five years—you won't find it so gross then."

"Mom keeps saying that. I don't believe her." Otis gave her a little wave. "I'm going to bed. And Lucy? Thanks for driving me to camp."

With that, he closed her door behind him, and Lucy let out a sigh of relief. The last barrier to going out with Dylan was out of the way…and her brother was talking to her again.

Now, if she could just save Serena's farm, life would be perfect.

Chapter Twenty-Five

DYLAN

"Hey, you in there?" Tristan waved his glove in front of Dylan's face. "I asked if you want to practice this afternoon."

Camp had gone by in a blur, punctuated only by a quick hello and good-bye to Lucy. Joking around with her last night had launched him out of bed this morning, wondering what the hell she had planned for tonight. Otis had even talked to him, though he was a little shy, like he didn't know where he stood. Dylan had focused a fair amount of attention on him, so he knew everything was cool. For the rest of the day, his mind kept wandering to the marina: the idea of dusk, singing cicadas, and a pretty girl with crazy ideas.

"Oh, sorry. I was just…yeah, I need to practice a little. I rested Sunday, so I should be rested enough, but shouldn't take chances." Dylan bent to pick up baseballs scattered all over the infield from the hitting practice the outfielders took against his pitchers that morning. "Let's grab some lunch."

Tristan squinted up at the sun. "Good plan. Even better—

Alyssa's dad updated the batting practice field behind their building. We could go up there and have her watch us."

"That's a good idea. Alyssa always sees things I miss." For once, saying her name didn't sting. Dylan took note of that. Lucy was good for him in more ways than one.

After a quick shower, they hit Snaps. Tristan raised an eyebrow when Dylan ordered a fruit plate and a chicken breast. "Dude, that's the saddest lunch I've ever seen."

"Hey," Kathy said. "It's better than the crap they serve in your school cafeteria. There's nothing wrong with healthy food."

"Sorry, Kathy." Tristan gave her a cocky salute. When she left, he shook his head. "Look, I know you don't eat many sweets, but isn't this taking things too far?" He held up a french fry. "You're missing out."

Dylan's stomach rumbled. "I only have twenty-four hours until my tryout. I'm leaving nothing to chance."

"Iron-clad discipline right there." Tristan munched another fry. "Good for you."

"Now you're just trying to make me feel bad." Dylan speared a piece of cantaloupe. He didn't love melon, but that's what was in season this time of year. He choked it down, shuddering. "Yum."

"That's the spirit." Tristan laughed. "You're going to be great tomorrow."

"Will you hit for me?" Dylan asked. "Maybe the scout will look at both of us?"

"Sure. Happy to. But even if the scout is interested, I want to give OSU a try." Tristan gave him a searching look. "If you change your mind, I bet a bunch of schools would come after you, too."

Dylan shrugged, pretending to be interested in a sad blueberry that had rolled under some honeydew. "We'll see."

"I'm just saying…and that's all I'll say. Hey, you want to

go to the lake this weekend? Alyssa has Sunday off for once." Tristan gave him a sly smile. "Lucy's invited if she wants to come."

That got Dylan's attention. After that awkward first meeting at the lake last week, it seemed so weird that he'd be inviting Lucy on a double date with his friends. "I'll ask her."

"Good. I like her for you, man. And I bet she's a blast to have around."

"You have no idea."

"You'll have to tell me sometime, then." Tristan grabbed the check before Dylan could make a play for it, and put some cash down. "Let's go practice."

"You're killing me, Smalls!" Alyssa called to Tristan. "Dylan's owning you right now. Those splitters are insane."

"Love you, too, gorgeous." Tristan rolled his eyes at Dylan. "Throw me a fastball so I can reclaim my manhood."

Dylan rolled his shoulders. The splitter had definitely come along, and Tristan couldn't hit it. Not at all. A showcase pitch, ready right when he needed it. But Tristan needed some fun, so Dylan wound up and threw a slower-than-usual fat fastball straight down the middle. Tristan smacked it with a satisfying *Ting!* and the ball soared over Dylan's head into the vacant field behind him.

"That felt good," Tristan said.

Alyssa stood on tiptoe to wrap her arms around him from behind. "Better. And Dylan? You're looking hot. That scout will be drooling, my friend."

Dylan couldn't keep the proud grin off his face. Alyssa knew pitches—probably better than anyone in Suttonville. She'd pitched softball for several years, but working in a batting cage facility gave you the kind of repetitive training most people never had. If she said he looked good…he looked good.

They let themselves back into the main building and walked to the front. From the way Tristan and Alyssa kept swaying toward each other, even doing something as simple as walking, Dylan knew he needed to go. "I'm going home to rest. Um, Lucy and I are going out for a little bit tonight, and I should clean up."

Alyssa smacked Tristan on the chest. "You didn't tell me they were a thing for real."

"I wasn't 100 percent sure myself." Tristan jerked his chin at Dylan. "Not until I caught them twining their fingers together through the fence at practice yesterday."

Dylan tugged at his collar, feeling a flush race down his back. "Yeah, well."

"Otis didn't look too happy," Tristan added. "But today he seemed fine."

"Yeah." Dylan paused. "I was a little surprised, but it was out of his system. Maybe Lucy talked to him."

"Good." Tristan slid an arm around Alyssa's waist. "I feel like a walk by the creek."

It wasn't so much what he said, but how he said it that seemed to cause a reaction in Alyssa. Yeah, Dylan was definitely leaving. "Have fun. And thanks for practicing with me."

"Good luck tomorrow." Alyssa gave him a swift kiss on the cheek. "You'll do great."

Smiling, and flushing even hotter now, Dylan waved and left for home.

At eight on the dot, Dylan settled onto the picnic table under the awning, watching for Lucy. He wasn't totally surprised that she wasn't here yet. Funny how quickly you can get used to a person's quirks. For him, early was on time, on time was late, and late was screwed. Lucy operated in her own concept of space-time.

Dylan laughed. Maybe Lucy really was an agreeable alien here to meet a human. It might explain some things. And who wouldn't want to hook up with a hot alien girl?

The lake was busy with boats of all kinds tonight. They dotted the gray-green surface, some shadowed with the coming sunset, others dashing across streaks of fading sunlight. Dylan had always loved the lake. It gave him a sense of peace. It never changed. It was always there. But something inside him chafed, wanting to be free. It wasn't like him to be restless. He'd like to blame it on the tryout, and the beginning of The Plan. He couldn't, though.

He was restless, waiting to see Lucy.

Then there she was, walking fast down the path to the picnic area, a box in her hands. She smiled at him, and it lit fuses up and down his spine. Dylan slid off the table, hands aching to reach for her.

She strode over, put the box on the table, then wound her arms around his neck. "Hi."

"Hi."

They stood there, inches apart, staring into each other's eyes, until Dylan couldn't take another second. He stepped closer and put his hands on her hips. He let one last second pass, then covered her mouth with his. Her leg brushed his, and he shivered. This was every bit as good as the beach Sunday. Better, even. He could kiss her for hours and still beg for more.

But she had plans and pulled back sooner than he would've liked. "Good to see you, too."

"Uh, yeah." Dylan blinked, trying to shake himself back to reality. "So, what do you have planned?"

"Anxious, are we?" She flashed him a coy smile. "It's nothing scary, if that's worrying you."

"So no streaking across the dock naked?"

"Man, I wished I'd thought of that." Lucy gave him an appreciative look up and down. "But, alas, no."

He flushed. Her eyes were sharp, and her gaze had made him *feel* naked. Not that he minded all that much. "That's disappointing."

She laughed and sat, hauling a canvas tote onto the table in front of her. Her face disappeared into it a minute before she reappeared holding a deck of cards. "This isn't the main reason we're here, but we need to kill a few hours, so I thought we could play cards."

A few hours? He should be getting a good night's sleep before the tryout tomorrow. What was happening at ten that they couldn't do at nine? Any other time, he'd let his imagination run wild, but tomorrow was too important. Still, he *really* wanted to know what she was up to.

She looked up at him, through her eyelashes. "Trust me."

That was enough. He took a seat across from her at the table. "What are we playing?"

"Gin. Whoever has the most points after ten hands has to do whatever the other person asks." She winked. "Just not *that*."

Dylan's ears burned. How'd she know "that" was exactly where his mind went? It was an idle thought—he was a seventeen-year-old guy, it was reflex—not anything serious, though. "Fair enough."

The breeze blew through the pavilion, drying the sweat on the back of his neck, and crickets started up in the trees. Lucy shuffled with the practice of a blackjack dealer and dealt the cards. Dylan sorted his, smiling. He already had three-of-a-kind, and a three card run. They were playing ten card hands, so he was off to a good start. What would he ask for when he won? For her to sit in his lap and kiss him senseless? That was a pretty good request. Or maybe to slow dance to the crickets? She might like that.

Lucy drew, watching him. He picked up her discard and tossed a card. She drew again, and he did as well. *Come on Jack of hearts.*

An eight. Dylan huffed and tossed it.

Lucy drew, then laid down her hand. "Gin."

Dylan's jaw dropped. "We drew three cards!"

She shrugged. "I'm good at this game. Maybe I should've mentioned that."

"Uh huh. Maybe I should shuffle this time, just to be sure." He took her cards, making sure to mix the deck up well. It didn't do him any good, though. She won in four draws.

After ten hands, Lucy won…by three hundred points.

"You set me up," Dylan said, not feeling too bad about it.

"Pretty much." Her smile promised all kinds of mischief, and he decided losing might not be so bad. "Come with me."

Swallowing down a hefty dose of nerves, he followed her down the path through the trees. He hadn't walked this trail before and had no idea where it led once they made it past the place where they danced in the rain. The trees were thick, and soon the pavilion disappeared from view. In here, it felt like the park was theirs alone.

After some twists and turns, and a quick duck under some brush, they came out at a little beach. Dylan looked around, frowning. He'd boated on this lake his entire life. How could he not know this was here? The cove was small, though. Too small for anything but a Sea-Doo, but close enough to the dock that people probably just overlooked it. He sure had.

"How'd you know this was here?" he asked, staring across the water, stained pink and orange by the sunset. The sun itself was a sliver of a disc barely above the waterline. It was probably almost nine, and it would be twilight any minute.

"And do you know how to get back in the dark?"

"Yes, I know how to get back." Lucy shucked off her sandals. "I found it a few years ago with my dad. I come out here a lot when I need time to myself. No one is ever here... and that makes it perfect."

The wicked, pleased note in her voice made him stand up straighter. "For...what?"

She held up a finger, watching the sun dip lower, and lower, until it was gone, and a blue-purple light fell across the lake. Then she raised an eyebrow and pulled off her shirt. She had a bikini top underneath it.

"I, um, I didn't bring a swimsuit," Dylan said, watching her wriggle out of her shorts. "I didn't know we were going into the lake."

Lucy didn't answer him, except to say, "Remember, I won the game."

Shock—the good kind—coursed through his veins. Just *what* did she have planned?

Once she had waded out into shoulder-deep water, she untied her bikini top and flung it up on the beach. Dylan stared at it dumbly, and her bikini bottoms joined the top. His brain went on full meltdown as he realized what she wanted him to do.

"Holy shit," he breathed. "Oh, holy, holy, holy shit."

"The water is nice and warm," Lucy called, smiling sweetly, as if she wasn't skinny-dipping in a very public lake, and expecting him to join her. "You coming in?"

That was the question, wasn't it?

Chapter Twenty-Six

Lucy bobbed in the water, wondering what was going through Dylan's head. She couldn't see his face, but she was pretty sure she'd blown a few of his brain cells and he had to think it over. She had faith his not-better nature would win out.

Another minute or two went by. Lucy whistled and paddled about, acting like she wasn't worried. In truth, her stomach was roiling. *Have I gone too far? Does he think I'm crazy?*

Then, he seemed to decide. He pulled his shirt off. Now she cursed waiting until twilight. She'd done that for the privacy, but she couldn't see.

"Turn around," he yelled.

Lucy choked on a laugh. "Seriously?"

"Maybe I want to keep you in suspense." There was a hint of a grin in his voice.

She turned around and stared at the darkening sky, delighted that he was going along with it. The gin game and impromptu skinny-dip wasn't the only thing she had planned for tonight, but it was a fun way to kill time. The Perseid meteor shower had started a few nights ago. They wouldn't see many—the main shower was in August—but she thought he'd enjoy sitting on the beach, away from city lights, watching for shooting stars.

Now, though, this part of the night might eclipse a meteor shower.

There was some splashing behind her, and a ripple of water rolled up over her shoulders. She smirked a bit as Dylan pulled even with her. He stayed a respectful three feet away, but it was pretty intoxicating anyway. He was taller, so his chest was out of the water, and she had just enough light to appreciate the hard angles of his shoulders and pecs.

"I can't believe I'm skinny-dipping."

"With a girl you hardly know?" she asked, thinking about his shock at kissing her the day after they met.

"In general." He threw his head back and laughed. It was the least stressed she'd ever seen him. He hadn't looked this carefree even on their date Sunday. Like she always said, a little chaos never hurt.

"Doing new things is good for you," she said, swimming around him, biting her lip to keep from laughing as his eyes followed her every move. He was going to try *really* hard to sneak a peek. Good luck with that. "Besides, isn't the water nice?"

"Yeah, it is." He vanished from view, before popping up a moment later to wipe water from his eyes. "Murky, too."

"Did you just try to check me out underwater?" She splashed him. "No fair. This is an imagination-only exercise."

"When I asked you about streaking around the dock, you considered it, didn't you?" he asked, paddling after her.

She shrieked and swam out farther, but Dylan, with those strong arms, caught her easily. He grabbed her foot, and pulled her under, letting her surface less than a foot away from him. They shared a somewhat shocked glance and drifted apart.

"So, um, do you take many guys skinny-dipping?" he asked.

"No." She paddled back toward the beach, and he kept pace with her. "Just you. You're the first person I've ever brought here."

When she reached a place where her feet could touch, she stopped. Her chest was a tangle of nerves. It wasn't often she felt shy, but admitting he was the only one she'd brought to her little beach—and then getting naked with him—had rattled her confidence. Especially since it wasn't an invitation for sex, just for some risqué fun to see if he'd rise to the challenge.

Boy, had he.

He floated up next to her. "Thanks."

He sounded completely sincere. He must understand, then. She smiled up at him, then gasped. The show was starting. "Okay, this wasn't exactly what I had planned. My real plan for the evening is right over your left shoulder."

"What?" He turned, looking at the trees.

She risked popping out of the water and reached around his shoulders to tilt his head up just as another meteor streaked across the sky. "Shooting stars. See?"

"That's amazing." He glanced over his shoulder to smile at her. Lucky thing she'd made it back under the water. "This is great."

"Even the naked part?"

"That took some getting used to, but yeah, even the naked part." He laughed. "If any of my friends knew I'd gone skinny-dipping with a cute girl and didn't make a move, they'd never let me live it down."

"You can make a move…" When Dylan stiffened, his eyes wide, she laughed behind her hand. "*After* we put our clothes back on."

He nodded, then craned his neck to stare at the sky. They watched four or five more meteors flame out overhead before Dylan got out. She kept her back turned, and her bikini top plopped into the water right in front of her. Her bottoms followed afterward, landing next to the top.

"Dylan? You should really consider pitching. You're aim is dead on."

He laughed. "Think so? Maybe I'll give it a try."

Once she had her suit back on—tying the top while swaying in the water was harder than she imagined—she called, "Okay for me to come out?"

"Yeah."

She turned and sloshed her way onto the beach. Dylan was sitting on a log, wearing only his shorts. "I, um, wanted to dry off some before I put my shirt on."

Lucy ran a finger along his biceps. "No complaints here."

She pulled her shorts on, and sat next to him. The rough bark prickled at the back of her legs, but her feet were buried in sand, and Dylan was next to her. She'd put up with a lot more than prickly bark for a night like this. "When we go back to the picnic table, I made you something. For luck tomorrow."

He put an arm around her shoulders and kissed the top of her head. "Want to go back now?"

"Not just yet." She tilted her face up to his. "I need to give you a good luck kiss first."

"Good plan." His arm tightened around her, and his other arm slid under the back of her knees. She barely had time to yelp before he pulled her into his lap. "You want to know what I was going to ask you to do if I won the gin match?"

He nuzzled at her ear, and Lucy had a hard time focusing. "Uh…what?"

"This." His lips trailed down her neck. "And this."

"Your idea was better than mine, then." She felt her eyes grow heavy, and she leaned hard against him. "Much better."

"Let's call it a tie," he whispered, before kissing her softly.

A tie. A tie was good. She kissed him back, harder, and the tension in his body drained out. Pretty soon, they were going to tumble to the beach, too entwined to stay upright. Lucy didn't think that would be such a bad thing. She'd kissed three other guys. Done more than that with two of them… and everything else with one. Despite that, none of them had ever made her see sparks behind her eyelids the way Dylan was right now.

When he pulled away to kiss her jaw, her neck again, and down to her collarbone, she murmured, "I'm glad we met."

"Me, too," he said against her skin. He looked up, meeting her eyes, his expression surprisingly intense. "You make me crazy, Lucy Foster. And I mean that in a good way."

She ran her fingers through his hair. "Ditto."

He laughed and kissed her again, before sighing and setting her gently on the beach. "Much as I hate to break this up—and I really hate it—I need to get some rest before tomorrow."

"Yes, you do." She tossed him his T-shirt and pulled hers on as well. "But first, I need to give you your present."

They walked back to the picnic table hand in hand, and she motioned for him to sit before grabbing the bakery box. She'd spent two hours working in the kitchen that afternoon, but it had been worth it. She opened the box with a flourish. "Dark chocolate cupcakes with chocolate-amaretto cream icing."

Dylan's expression went funny. A little conflicted, and a lot of longing. That was a weird reaction to baked goods. "They aren't poisonous. Or full of weed. I swear."

"It's not that." After a pause, he sighed and said, "What the hell. Those look amazing."

He took a cupcake, and Lucy watched, grinning, as he ate it in four bites, before groaning. "Jesus, those are the best cupcakes I've ever had." He reached for another but stopped. "Are they both for me, or am I being a pig?"

"They're both yours. I have more at home. Mom and Otis wouldn't let me get away without making some for them, too." She pushed the box toward him. "Have at it."

He snatched the cupcake out of the box. He took more than four bites to eat this one, but he ate it with a desperation that Lucy found hilarious. When he was done, he patted his stomach. "Thanks. Really."

"You're welcome." She reached up to wipe away a tiny bit of frosting at the corner of his mouth, before getting a better idea and kissed it away instead. He tasted like good chocolate, almonds, and vanilla.

She'd have to make him cupcakes more often.

Then she was in his lap again, and they were kissing with the same kind of intensity they had at the beach. His hand tangled in her hair, and she ran hers up his back under his shirt. Dylan's breath caught as her fingers skimmed along his spine. Thoughts flitted through Lucy's mind, hard to hold onto. Mostly that she felt like this was where she belonged. She wished she could stay out here all night.

They were both breathing hard, mouths hungry and searching. Dylan's other hand traced the line of skin between her shorts and T-shirt, and she whimpered against his mouth. Did he have any clue what he was doing to her?

His answer was to pull her closer and run his hand up her back under her T-shirt. She smiled against his mouth. *I'm such a bad influence.*

Just when his fingers brushed against the string tying her bikini top, a light swept across the tables, and several high-pitched giggles rang out. Dylan snatched his hand out of her shirt like he'd been burned, and Lucy slid off of his lap, shading her eyes. Five Girl Scouts, probably about ten, were shining a flashlight right at them. Lucy heaved a sigh. "Shoo! I'm sure you aren't supposed to be wandering around by yourselves."

"That was so gross," the girl with the flashlight said, and giggles erupted again.

The group walked off, their voices high as they discussed what they saw. Lucy rolled her eyes. "They'll get a hundred miles out of that story, I'm afraid."

Dylan laughed uncomfortably. "All the same, it was probably good they showed up when they did. I was…um… yeah."

She heard what he didn't say. She was both relieved and frustrated. "We should go, then. You need your beauty sleep."

He helped her carry her bag to her car, giving her a soft, sweet kiss before heading to his own. He waited until she pulled out and followed her Jeep to the park gate. Once there, they turned in different directions. Lucy felt an ache behind her breastbone.

She missed him already.

Chapter Twenty-Seven

DYLAN

Dylan woke up, saw what time it was, and scrambled out of bed. He'd overslept for camp twice now. What the hell? And today of all days?

As he rushed through getting ready, his mind wouldn't stay focused. He'd had a lot of trouble going to sleep the night before, thinking about Lucy. The way she smelled, the way she felt in his arms. The way she did whatever popped into her head without fear or remorse. Who knew skinny-dipping without contact could be so fun? Or so damn hot? Jesus.

Now, though, he was late. He ran through the kitchen, grabbing a protein bar and sending a hurried wave his mother's direction. He'd had the sense to pack his gear bag yesterday and had left it at the stadium to be sure he hadn't forgotten anything. Still, he didn't like how unsteady he felt as he drove the speed limit all the way to Suttonville High. Late or not, two tickets in less than a week would result in the loss of his car keys. His parents were annoyed enough by the first one.

Tristan shot him a questioning look when he jogged onto the field, heading for the knot of pitchers. Dylan threw up his hands in the universal sign of, "I know, I know," before turning to his campers. "Hey guys, sorry I'm late. Have you done your warm up run?"

Nods all around. Otis raised his hand. "Coach Tristan told us to run with his group."

Good thing someone was looking out for him—and his little guys. "Good. Then let's stretch. I'm going to stretch with you today."

The boys exchanged looks, even as they sat on the grass to start hamstring stretches. "Why?" Jacob asked, and all at once, ten sets of eyes were focused on Dylan.

He smiled. "I'm pitching for someone after camp this afternoon. I need to loosen up some."

"Like a scout?" Otis asked, looking mischievous.

Someone's sister must've been talking at home. Dylan nodded. "Like a scout. Now let's halt the chitchat and get started. Everyone, deep breath in, deep breath out..."

The boys were unusually attentive the rest of camp. Better behaved, too. Dylan didn't think it was anything he'd done— more likely the news of his tryout had given him some cred where the campers were concerned. Funny how that worked. At first, he felt like he'd burst with pride at each awed look. As camp went on, Dylan's stomach soured and his head hurt. Nerves? Well, no crap, he was nervous. But this felt a little worse than typical "big game" butterflies.

The boys stayed to clean up, some of them obviously stalling. "The tryout is later today, guys," Dylan told them. "And closed to the public."

A round of "awwwwws" went through the group, and the boys ran for their rides. Otis lingered, though. "Was I not supposed to tell them?"

"It's a little bit bad luck," Dylan admitted. "But if things go well, I'll tell you all about it tomorrow, first thing."

Otis nodded, his ears pink and his eyes worried. "Good luck, Coach Dylan."

"Otis!"

Dylan looked over at the fence. Lucy was wearing a pink T-shirt that matched her hair, and ripped jean shorts. He smiled and waved, then sent Otis over. She waved back, waiting, but when she realized Dylan wasn't going to come see her, she shrugged and took her brother to the car.

"Why'd you blow her off?" Tristan asked.

"I'm distracted enough," Dylan said. "I know that sounds stupid, but she's been on my mind a lot and I need to get my shit together."

Tristan checked his phone. "We have time to shower and run to Dolly's for a quick bite, if you want."

Dylan rubbed his stomach. His head hurt worse and the thought of food made him want to hurl. "You can go. I'm going to stay here."

"You need to keep your strength up." Tristan frowned. "I'll bring you something."

Dylan didn't think saying no would change anything, so he followed Tristan to the dugout. Why did his stomach hurt so much? He'd done so well with his diet the last few—

"The cupcakes." Sighing he dropped onto the bench and bent over, taking shallow breaths. This happened to him sometimes, when he shocked his system with too much sugar, like at the holidays. He never should've eaten them.

Tristan was already on his way to the showers, but he stopped. "What cupcakes?"

"Lucy made me good-luck cupcakes. They looked really good. They *were* really good, and I didn't want to be the jerk who didn't eat his home baked gift." Dylan forced himself to sit up. "Don't bring me lunch. I'm going to eat some ginger drops to settle my stomach."

Tristan nodded, his forehead wrinkled with worry, and went to shower. Dylan breathed in through his nose and out through his mouth a few times before going to Coach's office for the med kit. His mom had always given him peppermint for an upset stomach, but he'd found out ginger worked better when he started playing for Suttonville. Coach might be old school, but he knew what he was doing.

By the time Tristan got back, Dylan had showered, stretched again, and was sipping water.

"The scout's here," Tristan said. "Out in the parking lot, talking to Coach."

A thrill of fear and excitement ran down Dylan's back and into his arms and legs. Forcing himself to breathe, he nodded and picked up his glove. "Let's go get some practice swings in."

They went outside and Dylan threw five pitches. The first was a little wild. Tristan hit the next two, but Dylan managed strikes after that. By then, Coach and a man in khaki's, a blue polo with the red T logo for the Rangers, and expensive sunglasses were making their way onto the field.

"Dylan, this is Sam Hollister," Coach said, calm as ever. "Sam, meet my ace."

Dylan felt a surge of pride at that introduction and reached out to shake the guy's hand, mood instantly changing to embarrassment as he realized how sweaty his palm was. "Nice to meet you, sir."

"Likewise. Rick told me a lot about you. Seems baseball runs in the family." Sam gave him a friendly smile. "What pitches do you have?"

"Fastball, curve, changeup and splitter."

"A splitter?" When Dylan nodded, Sam said, "Impressive. Start with the fastballs. Is that your batter?"

"Yes, sir. One of the best on the team. He and I practice

against each other a lot." Dylan pointed, and Tristan waved.

"That's not a boast," Coach said. "Murrell there is pretty steep competition for any pitcher."

"Okay, good." Sam walked to a spot between third and home, probably to check out Dylan's form. "Let's see it."

Dylan wiped his sweaty hands on his pants, alarmed to see them shaking. He could do this. He just had to focus. He closed his eyes.

And Lucy promptly intruded, smiling and murmuring, *Do a good job.*

Right, he should keep his eyes open. He took a deep breath, let it out, and wound up. His first pitch was nice and hard, but high and outside. Tristan made a valiant swing at it—something he'd never do in a game. The pitch was a ball, through and through. The swing was to make the pitch look better than it was.

"Again," Sam called.

Dylan took another breath. His head was starting to hurt again, despite the sunglasses he'd put on with his baseball cap. *I can do this.* He wound up and threw. This one was more on target, but the speed was off, and Tristan hit it nice and square, sending it over the back fence. He mouthed *sorry*, and winced.

Sam paced a few steps. "Settle down, Dennings. This isn't life or death. One more fastball for me."

This time, Dylan managed a respectable fastball that went down the middle, and Tristan missed it honestly. Tristan gave him a quick thumbs-up.

"Okay, changeup." Sam said.

The changeup was Dylan's best pitch. He nodded and rolled his neck. This was where he would shine.

Except the first pitch he threw was in the dirt. Tristan's eyes went wide in a *what are you doing?* expression. Dylan shook his head and picked up another baseball from the pile at the back of the mound.

"Let's see that again," Sam said.

Dylan threw again, and Tristan only managed to tip this one foul. Better, but still not what he could really do.

"Let's move on to the curve."

Dylan gripped his new baseball tight. He'd been hoping for another chance at the changeup. Instead, he nodded, and he went back to his place. The curve and the splitter were more advanced pitches, and with the way he was throwing, this could be a disaster.

Swallowing hard, he wound up and threw a mediocre curve. Tristan swung early, so he missed it, but anyone with eyes would see that it was a bad pitch. Sam twirled a finger in the air, indicating he wanted to see another one.

This one was slightly better, but not big league stuff. Hell, it was barely single-A farm league stuff.

"Okay, splitter."

Dylan had to wipe his hands on his pants again. He'd only mastered this one in the last three weeks. He forced himself to center, to breathe. *You can do this. You can do this.*

And he did it all right—so off-speed and off-target that he hit Tristan in the thigh.

"Gah." Tristan crumpled to the dirt, holding his leg.

"Ooh." Sam winced. "That's gotta smart."

Dylan jogged over. "Oh my God, I'm so sorry."

"I know," Tristan said through gritted teeth. "Give me a sec, and I'll be up to try again."

The bravery in that statement put a lump in Dylan's throat. But no matter how much Tristan was willing to give, Dylan just didn't have it today. "Coach? Can you get Tristan some ice?"

Coach bent to help pull Tristan up. "Think that's it for today, Murrell. Dennings, I'll leave you to chat with Mr. Hollister."

Coach's voice didn't hold a trace of disappointment or

frustration, but Dylan knew he felt both…Dylan did, too. He trudged over to Sam. "Sorry. I must be tired from teaching little league camp or something. I…I'm usually much better than this."

Sam nodded. "I've seen tape from State, and I know you have good stuff. Look, you're going to have a major league arm someday. I don't doubt that a bit. But you need more seasoning before you throw yourself into the farm system. Don't take this the wrong way…but college ball will give you some refinement. That's the way you should probably go. You'll make it to the show, just don't rush things, okay?"

"I understand," Dylan said, not sure how to feel. Numb, mostly.

Sam patted his shoulder. "Work out for another few years, and I'll come back for a look. That splitter has some promise, once you iron out the accuracy issues. A good college pitching coach would put that to rights in a season, I bet. I'll, uh, see myself out."

He went to the gate out by third plate and disappeared into the parking lot. Dylan watched him go, seeing The Plan following behind him. Everything he'd worked for, focused on, giving things up for…gone. His parents would get what they wanted—their kid, in college, his life on hold while he waited for his dream to come true.

Dylan walked over to the dugout and sat. What had happened? Sure, he got nervous when it was a big game, but he mostly kept it together. This…*this* had been a shit-storm. He'd lost all control right at the moment he needed it most. Why? There had to be some reason he suddenly lost his focus…

But the only new variable in his routine had been Lucy.

Chapter Twenty-Eight

"Anything?" Otis asked, following Lucy from the kitchen to the living room, and from the living room down the hall to her bedroom.

She forced a smile. "For the eighth time, nothing yet."

Otis's shoulders slumped. "He said something. About me telling everyone being bad luck. Do you think it went bad?"

"Even if it did, it wasn't your doing," Lucy said. "Maybe he's out celebrating."

Without her.

She glanced at her phone again. It was past eight. The tryout had been at one-thirty. She'd tried texting, but he hadn't answered, and now she was a little fed up with the suspense. She opened a text window to Serena: *I still haven't heard how Dylan's tryout went. I'm worried.*

S: *raised eyebrow emoji* *I would be, too. Maybe you should call him?*

Maybe she should. Lucy hadn't wanted to bother him, but the waiting was killing her, so she dialed his number. He didn't pick up, so she left a message. "Hey, it's me. Just checking in. How'd it go?"

Then she sat there, staring at her phone, as the minutes ticked by. Otis popped in and out, looking for news.

Finally, the little dots indicating a message from Dylan popped up. Otis had peeked his head around the door for the third time, so Lucy waved him in. "I think I'm about to have an answer."

"Good."

D: *Not well.*

Lucy and Otis exchanged a sad look, before she texted back: *Damn. I'm so sorry. Do you want me to come over, cheer you up?*

"You shouldn't curse so much," Otis said, looking over her shoulder, but he sounded so glum, Lucy didn't clap back.

"I feel bad for Dylan, is all. He worked really hard for that tryout." Knowing Dylan, he was probably brooding and licking his wounds. She needed to do something.

"You're right, though. He probably needs cheered up." Otis tapped a finger against his temple. "You...you could kiss him. Just this once."

Knowing how much it took for Otis to make that suggestion, Lucy hugged him. "You know...you might be right. At very least, I'll go check on him."

"Good." Otis started from the room, but paused in the doorway. "And Lucy? I don't mind so much if you go out with him."

Lucy smiled at his back as he scampered away, calling to Mom about cookies. Otis's blessing meant more to her than she'd realized. She wanted him to be happy. Dylan, too. If she could manage it, she'd see that both the boys in her life were.

L: *Hey, want me to come over? I think you could do with some cheering up.*

D: …

D: …

D: …

L: *You there?*

D: *I'm out with Tristan right now.*

Lucy frowned at her phone at his curt tone. *Rain check, then?*

D: …

The minutes ticked by, until half an hour later, Lucy was pacing her room, phone in hand. When it finally rang, she didn't even check who it was before answering. "Where are you?"

"Uh, Lucy?" It was Tristan.

"Oh, hey." She slumped on her bed, disappointed. "Are you out with Dylan?"

"Um, yeah." There was a conversation going on in the background. "We're at Nate's house."

"Dude, I think he's had enough," a guy said. "I'm cutting him off."

There was a rustle, and Tristan murmured, "Yeah, good plan."

Lucy cocked her head. "What's going on?"

"I didn't want you left hanging. It's…Dylan's not really in a good place to talk right now." Tristan's tone made it sound like he was talking about a particularly feisty toddler. "He's a little upset."

"A little upset?" a voice slurred—Dylan. "A *little?* I'm lots upset."

"Hey, that's enough, man. Let the grownups talk, okay?" Tristan said, muffled.

"Is he drunk?" Lucy asked, growing alarmed. Dylan— disciplined Dylan, *drunk?* "Where does Nate live? I'm coming over."

"No, you don't have to come over." Tristan sounded super uncomfortable. "He'll be fine. We're all mostly sober and can take care of things. I swear we won't be driving, either."

"Is she…asking to come over?" Dylan's voice held that belligerent edge that came with way too much alcohol. "Tell her *no*. She wrecked my career. I'm *done*."

A cold knot hardened in the pit of Lucy's stomach at his acid tone. "Wait, what did he say?"

"Ignore him," Tristan said firmly. "He's completely wasted and has no idea what he's talking about.

"Or maybe he's being brutally honest." Lucy clenched her fists. She was done being shocked. She was *pissed*. "Lots of things are starting to make sense now. Like how he seemed to have this internal struggle before eating a cupcake. I mean, who has to debate their conscience over a cupcake a girl baked with her own two hands?"

"Lucy, he's really drunk. I'm not kidding. He's done, like, five shots of Jack in less than thirty minutes. He has no idea what he's saying right now."

"*In vino veritas*," she said, her face flushed with anger.

"Uh, what?"

"In wine, truth. It's Latin. You jocks should give the classics a try." Lucy blew out a furious breath. "What I'm saying is that whisky makes us honest. He means every goddamned word he says."

"I think he's just grasping at straws, okay? He had a really bad day, and he hasn't come around to accepting it, yet." Tristan sighed. "Lucy, please, don't blame yourself."

"I'm not blaming myself!" she shouted. "If he wants to blame me, fine. I don't have to listen to it."

"Then don't!" came Dylan's return shout. He'd heard her through the phone. "My life was…fine…before you came around."

"It wasn't fine! It was totally boring!" She let out a growl. "Fuck you, Dylan Dennings."

"You wish!" he slurred. "Skinny-dipping? Really?"

All the rage drained out of Lucy, leaving a cold shock behind. She swallowed back a sob— She had some dignity left and she damn well wasn't going to cry in front of him. "Go to hell."

"Lucy, wait—" Tristan said, panicked.

"Too late." Lucy hung up, lips trembling. Dylan blamed her for blowing his tryout. It had been one of the most important things in his life, and he blamed her for ruining it. Not only that, he made it sound like she was a dark star, sucking the good things out of his entire life.

Lucy pressed her fist against her mouth and sank onto her bed. Fat tears spilled over her eyelids and ran down her face. She'd been accused of many things—some of them true—but never "dream killer." The thing was, she couldn't even really understand what she'd supposedly done to deserve that title. He'd been so *relaxed*, so happy last night. Surely that would've helped, not hurt.

She ground her teeth together, pissed that she was crying in the first place. There wasn't a rational reason to blame her. Not one. And now she was getting mad. Who did Dylan think he was, blaming her for a bad tryout?

Well, screw him. Screw all of them. She'd been right all along. Dylan wasn't her type, and neither were baseball players in general. At least now she knew.

With a wordless growl, Lucy punched her pillow, turned out her light, and made herself go to sleep.

The next morning, Lucy drove Otis to the ball field in stony silence. Otis kept giving her worried looks before asking, "Okay, what did I do?"

They stopped at a red light, and Lucy slumped. "Nothing. Nothing at all. Dylan is just being a...a...*boy*."

"Did you go see him last night?"

She shook her head. "I was told not to by his friends. He's...mad right now."

"Well, yeah. He didn't do good for that scout." Otis fiddled with his seatbelt as Lucy started through the intersection. "Don't be too mad at him, okay?"

"Can't promise you that." She gave him a sidelong look before refocusing on the road. "But I won't make a scene, either."

No, she was saving that righteous rage for her protest with Serena later. She needed a good fight, and she'd hold onto it for the hens' sake.

Otis didn't say anything until they made it to the drop-off line. "Drop me here. Don't park and walk me up. If Dylan is being a boy—and I'm not sure what that means—don't go in."

Lucy sighed. "Fine. I'll be back to pick you up at noon. Have fun."

"I will." Otis surprised her by giving her a quick hug. "It'll be all right. Promise."

She watched him sign in, then bound across the field to his friends. Before she pulled away, she caught sight of Dylan. He was standing on the pitcher's mound. When he saw her, he looked away.

Lucy drove off as fast as she could.

Chapter Twenty-Nine

DYLAN

Dylan felt a stab of guilt, deep in his gut, when he heard Lucy's tires squeal a little in the parking lot. He couldn't remember, exactly, everything he'd said last night, but he'd been told pretty firmly that he'd been a complete and utter asshole. His guilt was only made worse when Otis stomped over to him, one of his fists clenched, and a fierce, overprotective look on his face.

"What did you do to my sister?" he asked, bold as day.

"Why do you think I did something to your sister?" he asked, trying to stay calm.

"Because she wanted to go see you after your tryout, but his friends said you didn't want to see her, and she said you were acting like a boy. I don't know what that means, but it sounds bad, and now she's sad, and it looks like she's been crying, and if you made her cry, I'm…I'm going to kick you in the shins."

Otis paused to draw a deep breath, like he wanted to

continue his tirade, but Tristan appeared behind him and put his hands on his shoulders. "Buddy, why don't you come warm up with my guys for a bit, until you cool off. You're right… Dylan is acting like a dumbass, but kicking his shins won't solve any problems." Tristan shot Dylan a dark look over Otis's head. "Trust me. I tried it already."

Dylan rubbed his temples as Tristan led Otis away. The headache had persisted since yesterday…or maybe that was the hangover. He'd woken up on Nate's living room couch, disoriented, to find Nate standing over him with a cup of coffee, four ibuprofen, and an irritated expression. He'd handed the coffee and tablets to Dylan without a word, then left the room.

That was the first hint that his friends were more than a little pissed with him. The second had been Tristan's dressing down in the locker room before camp. His ears were still ringing with that one.

Now Otis. That one had him puzzled and embarrassed. Otis didn't seem to know much, but he knew something was wrong. Which meant Lucy was really upset…which meant Dylan had a giant problem.

Because in the harsh light of morning, and the painful ache of a hangover, he knew, in no uncertain terms, that he'd been a raging asshole.

It wasn't Lucy's fault. He'd been upset and looking for something to blame. That's what Tristan had said, and slowly the truth had sunk in through his aching head. He'd wanted to control his destiny for so long he'd forgotten that destiny doesn't like to be controlled. The baseball gods knew that. He should have, too. He'd had a bad day yesterday, and the slightest bit of bad luck could torpedo your shot—hadn't Rick told him that? The scout had said he was good, good enough for the majors, even, but that he needed more time to develop his arm. That didn't mean never. It just meant not right now.

The Plan was still alive… It was just delayed, was all. If he hadn't been so fucking defensive, maybe he wouldn't have blamed Lucy for everything. She wasn't the problem.

He was.

Now, he was stuck wondering if he'd figured it out all too late. Had he missed his chance to play in college?

Had he lost Lucy because he'd been too stupid to realize what he had?

"Kid, you don't look so good." Coach came up alongside him, watching the pitcher group stretch. "Maybe you should take today off."

He'd never done that before—given Dylan an out. And Dylan had never left in the middle of something. He stuck things out, didn't shirk, didn't quit.

But that was the old Dylan. The one who didn't need anyone, who always came through no matter how much pain he was in. Tristan had hitched his star to Alyssa, taking her advice and improving his swing because he listened.

And what had Dylan done? Chased off the first girl who made him feel like himself, who'd broken through the walls he'd put up.

"You know what? I think I'll take you up on that." He nodded to Coach. "I'll see you tomorrow."

He headed to the parking lot without a backward glance. Tristan had told Lucy what happened. Dylan had no idea what Tristan had said, but that didn't matter. She knew…so what mattered was apologizing and explaining that he didn't believe it, not really. He'd ask her out to lunch, and if she said no, he'd get down on his knees and beg if he had to.

Not even bothering to go home and change out of his workout gear, he drove straight to Lucy's mom's shop. Lucy's Jeep was there, so he parked and went around front. Trying to see where she was, he peered through the front door. A group of older ladies were seated at long tables, heads bent over fabric or sewing machines. Lucy's mom was going from table to table, checking things out.

Lucy wasn't in view.

Steeling himself, and realizing, belatedly, he was wearing cleats, he stepped inside.

A little bell tinged when he opened the door, and every head turned to look at him. Dylan brushed some dirt off his shorts and asked, "Um, is Lucy here?"

Her mom gave him a cool look. "She's in back. She might not want to see you, though."

The older ladies glanced at each other in delight. A soap opera was developing right there in the middle of the quilting shop.

Dylan stared at his shoes and nodded. "If she doesn't, I'll leave."

He made his way past the tables, grateful to push through the curtained doorway at the back of the room. Lucy was hunched over a piece of bright pink fabric, sewing something by hand. He cleared his throat, but she didn't stir.

Dylan couldn't tell if she was ignoring him, or so engrossed in her work that she hadn't noticed, so he walked over to stand in front of her table.

"You're in my light." Her tone was flat.

Ignoring him, then. Dylan sidestepped. "Sorry. Look, I wanted to see you, to explain…"

"To explain why you think I ruined your tryout? Why I ruined your *life?*" She met his gaze. Her eyes were dark with anger. "Don't bother. I deserve better than that."

"You do." He clenched his hands into fists to stop them from shaking. This wasn't going well at all. Even if he didn't remember everything, he'd obviously messed up more than he realized. "And that's why I'm here. To say I'm sorry, and that I *don't* blame you. It's all on me. The scout said I need more time. I think I was more mad that my parents were right, and that I need to go to college for a few years first. I never would have said any of those things if I hadn't been drinking."

"People tend to be honest when they're drunk." Lucy set the fabric down. "And I appreciate the apology, but I don't think this is going to work. I want to be with a guy who values what I bring to the table, not constantly questions the things I do. You had an epiphany, and so did I. I need someone who can handle spontaneous behavior, and you think I'm bad luck…it's not going to work."

Her expression was neutral, completely composed, but Dylan heard the raw hurt under the words. She must believe he didn't think she was good enough for him. In truth, she was probably too good to be true, in his case, anyway. "I don't believe that. If you'd give me another chance, I'd—"

Lucy picked up her work and started sewing again. "I have more important stuff to worry about today. Like the fact that Serena's farm is about to be closed, and I need to finish up these pieces to be auctioned off so we can send the chickens someplace other than a commercial farm."

He stood there, watching her sew, waiting for her to say something else. Finally, he nodded. "I wish you'd change your mind. If you do, I'll be waiting. You, uh, you have my number."

He turned and walked out the back door. He could tell she was hurt, but also that she still cared about him. He didn't know how he knew, but it was obvious. She was angry and upset, but no matter what she said, he didn't think she'd given up.

So he wouldn't, either.

Chapter Thirty

Lucy

Lucy wiped a shaking hand across her brow as soon as the door closed. The rational part of herself — the part she almost never listened to, usually to her regret — was telling her that no matter how she felt right now, she and Dylan were too different to ever work out for long. That ending it today was for the best, and would save some pain later.

The heart-led part of her was sobbing its eyes out.

She sighed and tried to finish embroidering the bear on the edge of the skirt she was working on. It was toddler size and perfect for a fifties sock hop costume. If she and Serena failed with their protest today, plan B was to raise money to help Serena's family move the chickens to private, free-range farms. She probably wouldn't make enough, but Lucy had gathered up every piece of work she had that wasn't spoken for and started posting it online in one of those charitable auction sites. If by some miracle the town chose to grant Serena's farm an exception, they could use the money to build misters around the pens to keep the birds cooler in the summer.

Serena had texted earlier to check on her, and Lucy had insisted she was fine. But when her mom dismissed her quilting class and came back, asking, "So?" in a soft tone, Lucy put the skirt down and covered her face with her hands.

"Oh, honey." Her mom's wrapped her arms around Lucy's shoulders. "You know, it looked like he ditched camp to come see you. That has to count for something."

"Not enough." Her words came out muffled and choked. "He feels bad now, but he's never going to see me the same way. I'm not enough. What he's looking for, no girl can fix."

"People say very stupid things when they're hurt." Mom bent to kiss the top of her head. "But I'll pick up Otis today and drive him tomorrow, if you want."

Lucy dropped her hands and nodded. "Thanks."

The front bell dinged, and Mom bustled out to tend to the customer. Lucy picked up the skirt a third time, trying to drown out the hurt with mind-absorbing detail work. Put the needle into the fabric, pull it through, repeat, repeat, repeat.

And it worked, until the needle slipped free and jabbed her in the thumb. Lucy stuck it in her mouth to staunch the bleeding and went to the bathroom. The hole was pretty deep, but it would mend. Kind of like the hole in her heart. She was hurt, but she'd mend.

She had to.

By the time Mom returned with Otis, the bear skirt was done, and Lucy was sewing a beak onto a yellow duck made with fuzzy thread and feathers. This one was a baby's bathrobe, made of soft, butter-colored terrycloth. Mom looked at it and chuckled. "That's cute enough to make me want another baby."

"No," Otis and Lucy said together. Lucy, because she remembered how sick her mother had been with Otis. Otis, probably because he was too used to being the baby himself. Lucy smiled at him. "How was camp?"

Otis glowered. "I yelled at Coach Dylan, then his Coach came over and sent him home. Maybe he was in trouble. He *should* be in trouble. No one messes with my sister."

Otis's chest was puffed out, and Lucy bit her lip to keep from chuckling…or crying. Or both. "Thanks for defending my honor."

Otis gave her a regal nod and went to the counter to microwave some chicken nuggets. Mom watched him go. "He's growing up. And he's very overprotective of you."

"He is. I'm just glad he's not mad at me for attempting to go out with Dylan." Lucy sighed. "I have plans with Serena this evening. Is that okay?"

"Definitely. You need friend-time."

Mom said it so warmly Lucy instantly felt guilty. If they got arrested, how would Mom feel? Hopefully, she'd see it was for a good cause.

Or she might ground Lucy for a year. At least that way she wouldn't have to worry about seeing Dylan again.

Not much of a bright side.

"You're sure about this?" Serena asked, scanning the street in front of Town Hall. It wasn't very busy, but it would be soon. The meeting started in forty-five minutes.

"Yes." As the afternoon had worn on, Lucy's frustration and anger over…well, *everything,* had hit the boiling point. She was spoiling for a fight, and this one might actually do some good. "Let's go."

They hauled the large crates full of straw out of the back of Lucy's Jeep and lugged them over to the sidewalk right by the stairs leading up to the Town Hall building. Signs on sticks rested in the straw, ready to be held up. She and Serena wore custom T-shirts—embroidered, of course—that said "Save Our Chicks" with a baby chick peeking out of a hatched egg.

Lucy spread a towel onto part of the straw and sat down in her "nest." The idea was to have the boxes look like nesting stations in a hen house. They'd spray painted things onto the wood like, "Vote for Chicken" and "Got Eggs? We Do." The signs, which Serena had made up, both said, "Save the Chickens. Vote Free Range!"

Slowly, people started coming down the sidewalk as Lucy and Serena chanted, "Save our chicks! Save our chicks!" A lot of people chuckled at the display, and a few nodded. One old lady with a cane said, "Are you from Blake farm? I love your eggs. Best in town."

Serena had given her a brilliant smile. "Yes, they are. But if the town closes us down, you won't be able to buy them anymore. They're voting tonight on whether or not we can stay."

"Closes you down? That's ridiculous." The older lady started for the stairs. "I'm going in to find out what's what."

And older gentleman followed her, tipping a worn-out fedora.

But not everyone was supportive. As the meeting time grew closer, some council members eyed them with distaste, and an aide came out to hassle them. The woman couldn't have been more than twenty-three, dressed in a pencil skirt and black heels. "Girls, do you have a permit? If you don't, you'll need to move on."

Lucy sat up straighter. "You're about ten minutes older than I am. Where do you get off calling us 'girls'?"

The woman's eyes narrowed. "I'm going to ask you again. Where's your permit?"

"What permit?" Serena asked, angry. "This is frcc speech."

"Yes, but you need a permit, even if it's a peaceful protest."

The woman crossed her arms. "Are you going to go?"

"Nope." Lucy waved her sign at the woman. "We're here to save our chickens. You can't make us go."

"We'll see about that."

The woman *click-clack*ed off in her heels, and Lucy craned her head to watch her. The mayor was standing just inside the door, watching them.

"Do we really need a permit?" Serena asked, worried.

"No idea. We'll probably get a ticket, but we knew that already." Lucy sighed. "Let's keep this up as long as we can."

They shouted and waved their signs as more people went into the Town Hall building. When Serena's dad appeared, he groaned. "What are you two doing?"

"Peaceful protest, Dad," Serena said. "You have your part, we have ours."

He looked at both of them. "This might be taking things too far."

"You know us, Mr. Blake. If there's a line, we're on the wrong side of it." Lucy grinned. "Now go in there and give them a scolding. We've got your back."

Mr. Blake tugged at his bow tie, his suit looking all wrong on him. "Stay out of trouble. I'll be back in a bit."

Lucy saluted him as he walked up the stairs, then went back to chanting with Serena. They'd slowly gained a crowd, mostly people out for dinner downtown and not interested in the meeting. The sidewalk was full, and a few people were standing on the Town Hall stairs to have a better look.

Because they couldn't see around all the people, Lucy didn't notice the police officers until they'd pushed their way into the crowd. Okay, this was it, then. They were about to be cited and sent home. Ms. Pencil Skirt must've called them.

"Ladies, we're going to have to ask you to leave," the first officer said. "You're blocking the sidewalk."

"We aren't," Lucy said, her voice trembling. "The crowd

happens to be, but they aren't with us."

The second officer, younger and probably new, said, "Doesn't matter. You're violating rules of peaceful protest because you're blocking the sidewalk. Get up."

The first officer gave him a flat look before turning back to Lucy. "Come on now. Your parents wouldn't want you to be stirring up trouble. You look like good girls. Clear the area, and let's call it a night."

Good girls? That made them sound like a pair of spaniels. Lucy's frown deepened. She'd been so angry all day her filters had been turned off. Bad timing, but she couldn't make herself care. "No."

"No?" The officer's eyebrows rose. He reached for his citation pad. "The ticket for protesting without a permit is five-hundred dollars, young lady."

"Yes, but we're exercising our First Amendment right to speak against the town government. They're going to make the farm close." Lucy stood, her arms crossed over her chest. "It's not fair."

"You're breaking the law," the second officer said, taking a step toward her.

"Hey, now," a woman in the crowd called. "I'm recording this. Better watch out, Officer Friendly."

The younger cop scowled and held his ground. "Let's go. You know the rules. We're here to make sure you follow them."

Serena got up and started packing up her crate, but Lucy didn't budge. She'd had enough. "And what does following those rules get us? Seeing my friend's chickens shipped off to some butcher's farm to live in tiny cages and never see the sun? I love those chickens. They're sweet and they're happy where they are. The farm is barely inside town lines, and they don't have any next-door neighbors. This new ordinance is silly."

"Lu," Serena said, urgent. "Let it go. We've done what we came for."

Tears welled in Lucy's eyes. She couldn't give up. "Fine." She raised her voice. "Everyone here? Since we have to leave, go inside and tell the council to let the farm stay."

She hopped out of her crate, leaving it on the sidewalk, too angry and sad to pick it up. Lucy kept walking until a hand caught her arm. She stared up at the younger cop, surprised he'd grab her like that. "You can't leave the crate. Pick it up."

"But...but you asked me to go." At the edge of Lucy's vision, Serena stood on the sidewalk, looking worried. Was this the part where she got Tasered or something?

"I've got her crate," a man said, a complete stranger. He was about her dad's age, and he smiled at her. "And my wife went inside to petition for the farm."

The older cop came over. "Let go of her, Simons. Young lady, take this." It was a ticket. The officer frowned, almost apologetic. "The mayor insists that we cite you."

Lucy took the ticket with shaking hands, keeping an eye on the younger cop. That guy needed to change professions. She stared at it in confusion. "Littering?"

"He said to cite you without saying for what. I took that to mean it was up for interpretation. Run along home, now." The cop winked at her, then turned to Simons. "Let's go. Our shift's about over."

They turned to go, and Lucy glanced at the ticket again—it was for fifty dollars. Not five hundred. She snorted. "Well played, sir. Well played."

Once the man helped Serena load the crates into the Jeep, Lucy sagged against the tailgate. "Not sure if we did any good."

Serena pulled her into a hug. "Whether it worked or not, thank you. I was scared you were going to be arrested, though."

"Me, too." She shuddered. "That Simons needs to find a new job."

"I think his partner will straighten him out." Serena let Lucy go and looked toward Town Hall. "I wish we knew what was going on."

Lucy rolled her neck and bent to stretch her back. The tension from her run-in with the cops had knotted her muscles. "We could go in."

She laughed. "No. We might get arrested for real if we set foot in that building."

"Then we'll hang out here until your dad comes." Lucy went and rummaged in the back seat, returning with two bottles of water.

"Now that the excitement is over, are you going to tell me?" Serena asked between gulps. "Did Dylan say anything about his behavior last night, or are you two ignoring each other?"

"He came by, supposedly to apologize, but it's over." She forced a brave smile. "I'm good, though. It's fine."

"No, it's not." Serena sighed. "It's really not."

She didn't press for more answers, and Lucy was grateful. If she was going to worry, it needed to be about things that counted: chickens, her dad, her mom's health, and whether or not her auction would be enough.

Her heart didn't need to make room for anything else right now. No matter how much it ached.

Chapter Thirty-One

DYLAN

Dylan paced his room, wondering what else he could do. After his disaster of an apology to Lucy, he'd gone home and run on the treadmill for a solid hour. Instead of making him feel better—or at least numb—he'd only felt worse. Now he was practically crawling out of his skin, wishing he'd been less of a dumbass.

"You're going to wear out the floor," Tristan said, watching him pace. He'd been sitting in the chair at Dylan's desk for more than an hour, having shown up after Dylan failed to answer any of his texts.

"There has to be something I can do." Dylan rubbed a hand over his head. "When Alyssa was mad at you, what did you do?"

"That was a misunderstanding, not…" Tristan cleared his throat awkwardly. "I got help from her best friend."

Enlisting help from the best friend. Classic technique. "Think Serena would help me?"

"Not a chance." Tristan gave him a sad smile. "But Otis might."

Otis. Why didn't I think of that? "This morning, he was as pissed as I've ever seen a nine-year-old get. Clenched fists and all."

"Yeah, but there's some hero worship left there, I think. You could always bribe him." Tristan laughed. "Keller bribed me all the time to keep me off his back, or to help him with chores."

"That's...not a bad idea." Dylan picked his phone up from the bed. "Except...I don't know how to reach him."

"I'm disappointed in you." Tristan pulled his own phone from his pocket. "We have access to all the releases from camp, remember?" He tapped and scrolled for a few seconds. "Here's his home number."

Dylan swiped the phone from him and dialed the number, only realizing as it rang that he had no idea what he was going to say. Randomly jumping into action was Lucy's way of doing things...but he could learn, right? Spontaneous could be his new motto.

A boy answered after four rings. "Hello?"

"Otis? It's Dylan."

"Oh." The kid's tone was flatter than fresh-mowed grass. "What do you want? Lucy's not here, not that she'd talk to you."

"I'm calling to chat with you. I need your help. I want Lucy to start talking to me again, but I don't know what to do. What do you think will work? Flowers? Candy?"

Otis snorted.

"See why I need your help, then?" Dylan asked. "I don't bake, man. I can't sing, and I'm only good at throwing a baseball."

"That's not true," Tristan muttered, and Dylan threw a pillow at him.

"She likes chickens." Otis paused. "Serena's farm might be shut down. I heard Lucy talking about it. She's doing this web thing to make money. Like, selling her sewing stuff to people for donations."

"An auction?"

"I think so."

After a quick conversation with his mom, Otis was able to tell him the site address for the auction. Dylan typed it into his phone. "Thanks, buddy. Look, I might need your help to talk Lucy into meeting me. I promise I won't hurt her. Will you help me say I'm sorry again?"

"Well..." Otis's tone was crafty. "What's in it for me?"

He sounded like a child-mafia boss, and Dylan burst out laughing. "Lunch at Dolly's next week, and ten pitching lessons, on the house."

"Deal!" Otis said, much too quickly. "Tell me what to do tomorrow."

They hung up and Dylan hurried to his desk, shoving Tristan aside. "Dude."

"Sorry. I need my wallet." He fished out his credit card. He had almost two grand in the bank. Would that be enough? Hoping so, he started hitting "bid" on every single item in Lucy's auction.

Then he stopped to think—maybe two grand wouldn't be enough. He needed a partner or two. Most of the stuff was girly and cute, some of it for little kids. A slow smile tugged at his mouth. "And I need to text my grandma."

Chapter Thirty-Two

The wait was taking forever. The cops hadn't come back, but Lucy and Serena had retreated to the Jeep for some A/C and to avoid the mosquitos.

"That's one more thing," Serena had murmured, resting her head against the window. "Chickens eat mosquitos," she said before falling asleep. Lucy had plugged her headphones into her phone, too restless to nap…or even sit. She played Candy Crush, looked at Instagram, and watched a YouTube video to learn a particular stitch she wanted to try.

Even with all that, something had burned just beneath her breastbone, impossible to ignore.

I want you in my life, and I wish you'd change your mind. If you do, I'll be waiting.

Lucy's fingers hovered over her text app. Sitting here, not knowing what would happen to the hens, had left her lonely and in need of a hug. Dylan gave great hugs.

Had she been wrong? Her fingers twitched. Should she

let him back in, even if she'd probably end up hurt in the long run? Or should she swear off boys until college, where she'd be more likely to find someone more compatible?

Her index finger opened the text window under Dylan's name…what was she doing?

The door to Town Hall opened, and people began trickling out. The meeting must be over. Lucy silently thanked fate for saving her from a mistake and nudged Serena awake in the passenger seat. "Looks like it's breaking up."

They sprang out of the car to wait for her dad.

Lucy recognized the older lady who'd agreed with her on the sidewalk, and the man who'd carried her crate to the car, holding hands with a woman. Okay, they wouldn't be leaving if the council still hadn't voted about the chickens.

An excruciating five minutes later, Serena's dad came out. His collar was open, and the bowtie was gone. He walked with a man wearing khakis and a polo with some kind of logo on it. At the bottom of the stairs, they shook hands, and parted ways.

"Dad!" Serena called.

He turned and saw them, waving at a few more people as he came to the Jeep. He smiled at them both. "Well, I heard the police came."

"I was only ticketed for littering," Lucy said. "Nothing else."

"Huh." Serena's dad scratched his head. "That's good. I was worried I'd need bail money, and that your mother would ban us from seeing you ever again."

"Enough about that," Serena said. "What happened?"

"Well, my arguments weren't doing much good. One woman on the council really hates chickens—roosters in particular. All I can think is a rooster terrorized her when she was a girl." He rolled his eyes. "Nothing I said could convince her otherwise."

Serena drooped. "So we're losing the chickens."

Her dad held up a hand. "Now hold up, and let me finish."

Lucy and Serena exchanged a look: *What does that mean?*

"The man I was just talking to? He's from the state department of agriculture. I'd called them a few weeks ago, kind of as a last-ditch effort. Imagine my surprise when he showed up to the meeting." He laughed. "Anyway, he was there to sing the praises of free-range chickens and eggs, and to announce that he was working with a farmer's co-op to set up a farmer's market in town."

"Okay, so?" Serena asked.

"So it means that a lot of people will pay extra for organic eggs, and the state wants to encourage ethical farming." Now her dad was full-on grinning. "They gave me a special permit. They aren't changing their stance on chickens per se, but we're being grandfathered into whatever policy they decide. Now, the permit fees aren't cheap—that's the council's way of getting in one last dig—but if we pay it and submit to an inspection every year, we'll be allowed to keep the farm.

Lucy bounced on her toes, clapping, and Serena burst into tears. Her dad gathered her into a hug. "It's okay, honey. It's all right."

Lucy stopped bouncing, struck with a thought. "How much is the permit?"

"Two thousand the first year, and eight hundred each year after that, if we pass the annual inspection."

"Two *thousand?*" Serena's forehead wrinkled with worry. "Is this a play to make us reduce the size of our farm? We didn't profit that much last year and probably won't this year. How are we going to come up with the money and still afford to buy chicken feed?"

"We'll think of something," her dad said, but he sounded concerned, too. "We could sell the boat, maybe."

Lucy looked between them, knowing selling the boat

would hurt. Plus, while Mrs. Blake was happy to let Mr. Blake have the farm, she would only support it if the hens made enough money to sustain themselves. He and Serena had built up the farm a bit at a time to be sure they could pay for everything out of the profits from the eggs.

Lucy hoped she could help. She fished her phone out of her pocket. "I launched that auction thinking I could give you money for misters or to help move the girls if you couldn't keep them, but if I sell enough, I can help pay the fee."

Mr. Blake patted her shoulder. "Lucy, that's really kind of you, but we'll manage. Somehow."

She punched in the code to log into her auction page. "I love your farm, I love the hens, and I love you guys. It's only fair that I contribute."

"But you do." Mr. Blake sounded bewildered. "You help us out for nothing. You haul water and gather eggs. You do so much already."

Lucy waved him off, scrolling down the list of items. Every single one had a bid. A few had more than one. She sucked in a breath. "Um, guys?" She looked up at them, suddenly feeling like crying herself. "I've made eighteen-hundred dollars so far."

When she arrived home, Mom and Otis were waiting for her in the living room. Lucy stopped short. "What? I'm not late this time."

"Geez, Lucy! What happened to the chickens?" Otis asked.

"They can keep the farm." Even now, saying that made Lucy want to pump her fist in the air. *Suck it, Officer Simons.*

"That's great news." Mom yawned and stretched. "Well, I'm off to bed. Lucy, don't forget you're babysitting the quilting class so I can drive Otis."

Lucy's good mood faltered. "Okay."

Her mom smiled at Otis. "Are you all squared away for tomorrow?"

It was a question she'd asked him a hundred times during the school year, but the look the two of them exchanged before Otis's brisk, "Yep," had Lucy suspicious.

"Is something going on that I don't know about?"

"Oh, we're playing a game tomorrow. At camp. I'm starting for the blue team," Otis said, sitting up straighter.

"That's great, Squirt." A little part of her was sad to miss it. But she'd probably be a distraction—and distracted herself. "Good luck."

She went to bed, not sure how to feel. She was elated about Serena's farm, but doubt kept gnawing at her belly, asking if she'd done the right thing with Dylan. And where was this newfound caution coming from? Usually she never shied away from doing what she wanted, not giving one thought about the consequences. This summer had changed her. Maybe *Dylan* had changed her, too.

Sighing, Lucy dropped into sleep.

The next morning, Mom shook her awake. "You need to leave in ten minutes to be there early enough to prep before the shop opens. I'm leaving with Otis."

Lucy blinked, feeling slow and stupid. "Yeah, I'm up."

She hurried to throw on the first thing that seemed even remotely appropriate—striped leggings, with jean shorts and a T-shirt that proclaimed, "Sew Happy." The shirt had been her Dad's idea of a gag gift for Christmas last year, but she wore it all the time, so the gag was on him, really.

Mom had made coffee, and Lucy helped herself to a travel mug before dashing to the Jeep. Traffic was light, thank God, and she made it to the shop quickly. She started laying out the supplies right away, busily setting up machines and pulling down extra fabric squares. The materials were about ready when her phone buzzed on the counter. Lucy grabbed it and went to flip the shop's sign to "Open! Come on in!" before checking the message.

It was a direct message from the auction site: *Hello. I believe I won a number of items last night. I'm local to Suttonville. Could we arrange to meet for delivery?*

That was a good sign. Lucy checked to make sure the bidder had actually paid then replied: *Yes, how about this afternoon? I'm at the sewing shop on Main.*

The person messaged back immediately. *Excellent. See you…say two?*

L: *Sounds good.*

Shrugging, Lucy tucked her phone away and turned to greet Mrs. Jennings and prepare to start class.

Chapter Thirty-Three

"Do you think that sounded enough like what my mom would say?" Dylan asked Tristan, showing him the messages to Lucy about the auction.

"It sounds like what your *grandma* would say, dude." Tristan pointed at the sign in table. "Here comes co-conspirator number two."

Otis bounded over to them with long strides. "They saved the farm! So Lucy's going to give them money to pay some fee and to buy misters to keep the chickens cool so the hens won't get sick in the heat. Serena's favorite chicken, Sprinkles, died because she was too hot, and that made both her and Lucy really sad, so Lucy said she wanted to make sure it—"

"Whew," Tristan said, cutting Otis off. "You didn't even draw breath for all of that."

Otis rolled his eyes. "*Anyway*, everything is going good, so come to the shop, okay? Oh, and my mom knows, so she'll keep Lucy from leaving."

Her mom knows? Jesus. "Uh, thanks for that. I think."

Otis frowned. "Was our plan a secret, too? Oh, man."

"It's okay. Really." Dylan made a shooing motion. "Go get warmed up. We want to beat Coach Tristan's team, right?"

"Right!" Otis dashed off and Dylan let out a long breath.

Tristan gave him a light punch on the shoulder. "Don't worry. It'll work."

"This isn't a shirtless homerun derby," Dylan muttered. "What if she's mad I tricked her?"

"You didn't trick her. You're just getting your foot back in the door," Tristan said. "Now quit moping and get ready to coach your team."

Dylan nodded and went to the home dugout. He and Nate Rodriquez had done a coin toss against Tristan and Jeremy Ledecky for home-field advantage at the end of camp yesterday. Blue team had won, so they had the home dugout. Dylan took his place in Coach's usual spot. Coach was umpiring today, calling balls and strikes. The assistant coaches were umpiring the other three positions. It was kind of funny to see them out there with chest guards and black hats on.

The boys were noisy as they trooped inside, looking at him expectantly. Nate shrugged and said, "You're the coach. Give them a game day speech."

"Uh...you guys have come a long way the last few weeks," Dylan said, the back of his neck growing hot. "I've seen a lot of personal growth. Now let's go out there and see what we can do as a team."

The boys stared at him, then Otis shouted, "Yay, blue team!"

All the boys shouted it in return, and Nate snorted. "Is it sad that a nine-year-old can give a better amp-up speech than you can?"

"Shut up, Rodriquez." Although Dylan couldn't help laughing. He felt lighter today, after working out his plan to see Lucy, even if he was nervous about it. His talk with his parents last night about going to college had gone pretty well, too, and he was less upset about the idea with each passing day. Better to get encouraging news that wasn't exactly what you wanted, than news that you'd never get there.

The game started. Otis looked really good. He had his stance down, and his "game face" expression was so serious, Dylan nudged Nate. "Do I look like that when I pitch?"

"Man, I'm gonna take a picture next time. You're ten times worse. Other teams call you the Iceman. You know that?"

Yeah, he knew. And he'd probably stay that intense, but only on the field. He had some real living to do outside of baseball. Dylan stood and signaled to Otis to throw a changeup. They'd been working on these, and the kid had really improved.

Otis nodded, solemn, wound up, and threw a neat and tidy three-finger changeup, which was the beginner version of the pitch. The batter swung early—textbook—and struck out. Dylan gave Otis a thumbs-up.

In the end, blue team won. Otis struck out two of the three batters he faced before they let another pitcher have a turn. After they took a few pictures, Otis hung back. "I'll see you later, right?"

"Right. And Otis? I've enjoyed having you at camp."

The kid beamed. "Thanks." Then he was gone, and Dylan was left to set his plans in motion.

"Hey, good luck today," Tristan said when he came in to pick up his gear from the locker room. "And if all else fails, you could serenade her or something."

"If I ever sing to a girl, I'll be charged with war crimes." Dylan shoved his glove into his duffel. "No, I'll stick to being pathetic."

"You're anything but pathetic. She'll either say yes or she

won't. You're going places no matter what."

Dylan nodded to Tristan, glad their friendship had survived the Alyssa affair. He didn't know what he'd do without his best friend. Probably be pathetic.

Dylan ran home to take a quick shower and change clothes. His mother took one look at the boat shoes, plaid shorts, and aqua polo and choked on her salad. "Where on earth are you going, the yacht club?"

"Mom, you know we don't have a yacht club around here."

"Of course not, Chip," she said in a mock-snobby voice. "Tally ho."

Dylan threw up his hands. "I'm trying to impress a girl. Okay?"

Mom glanced him over again. "In that case, good showing. I can't believe you didn't try to give away that polo after grandma gave it to you last year."

Dylan scuffed a foot along the floor. "Me, neither. But this girl…she likes bright and shiny things. My closet is pretty boring, so this was the best I could do."

"Well, go see her, then." Mom smiled. "And if it works out, I'd like to meet her."

He nodded and went out to his car. Otis had texted that Lucy was hard at work in the back of the shop and to come in the front. *Mom will let you in.*

This was becoming a circus. He put his car in gear. If it didn't work out, he was going to slink out of that shop and hide in his mom's broom closet until graduation.

No, he wasn't going to think like that. He knew how to be determined and how to work for what he wanted. What he wanted was Lucy.

And he was going to fight to get her back.

Chapter Thirty-Four

Otis peeked out at Lucy from the playroom. She didn't even have to look up from the silk gloves she was embroidering with tiny skeletons to tell. The girl who'd ordered the corset for her Halloween party had stopped by with the gloves, asking Lucy to spruce them up. It was delicate work and required a steady hand.

Now her concentration was wrecked by the lurker who should be playing video games. "What, Otis?"

A *thump* and a chuckle. He was acting so weird, like he was in on a secret or something. But nine-year-old boys didn't have secrets, so whatever he was laughing at was probably related to farts or other bathroom humor.

Grinding her teeth, Lucy stitched the outline for the next skeleton. Its bones were so tiny, barely a few threads wide. She needed to concentrate, but she couldn't seem to do it. Maybe she needed a break, and she definitely deserved something sweet. Setting the work down, she stretched and called, "Mom, I'm going to the Wooden Spoon for some bread pudding. Want a piece of pie or something?"

"No!" Otis burst out of the playroom. "Don't go."

"Why not?"

His jaw worked, but Mom stepped in. "It's almost two. Isn't that auction buyer coming by?"

Oh, right. Damn it, she really could use some caffeine and a breath of fresh air to clear her head. "I'll wait."

Mom and Otis shared a look that set Lucy on edge. "Okay, what's going on?"

"Nothing," Otis sang.

Before Lucy could grill her mother in turn, the bell above the shop door rang. "Probably the buyer. I'll go."

"No, I'm up. I'll see who it is." Mom scurried out before Lucy could protest, and Otis slammed the door to the playroom. A moment later, the theme to his favorite superhero cartoon blared through the door. She was about to tell him to knock it off, when Mom said, "Lucy? I've brought the buyer back."

She didn't have a chance to wonder why her mom sent the buyer to the back before Dylan stepped through the doorway, the curtain falling back into place. Mom's footsteps receded to the front of the store.

"Why do I get the feeling I've been set up?" she asked. He looked good, dressed in a brilliant aqua polo that set off his tanned skin. "That's a great color on you. I didn't know you wore anything but Nike and Under Armor."

He laughed, self-conscious. "I'm trying to impress a girl."

"Ah." Lucy's face went red hot. "But what's this about the buyer? Did I not really sell anything?"

"No, you sold everything." He stared at his shoes. "I told my grandma about your auction. She loved your work, and my oldest cousin has two little girls. She had to outbid some lady in Oregon for that little ducky robe, but she beat her down."

A smile tugged its way across Lucy's face. "Are you serious?"

"Yeah. I heard about Serena's farm and wanted to help. My grandma loves this kind of stuff, so I called her. Whatever she didn't want…I, uh, bought myself."

"You bought a pink bustier with spider web needlework?" she asked. What was he up to?

"I bought it so I could give it back to you." He looked up, cheeks flushed. "I didn't think you'd accept a donation from me, so I won the auctions instead."

Lucy sat back in her chair. Her chest had gone tight, and it was hard to force air into her lungs. "You did all this…for Serena's chickens?"

"No." He took a step forward. "I did it for *you*."

Tears pricked the back of her eyes. "Why?"

"Because I thought it would make you happy." He frowned. "Should I not have done it? You love those chickens and I thought… God, did I mess up again?"

Lucy rose on shaking legs. "You did all this, just for me?"

"You wouldn't see me." His words were coming faster now, tumbling out. "I couldn't figure out what to do. I messed up so badly. Lucy, my tryout wasn't your fault— It was mine. I expected everything to go exactly like I planned, and it didn't. Then I acted like a big baby about it. I was so stupid. I lost you. It took me a while to realize that I need you in my life. You make me feel alive…and I didn't know I wasn't until I met you."

Lucy pressed a finger to his lips. "My turn, okay?" He nodded, looking scared and hopeful. She smiled crookedly. "No one's ever done anything like this for me before. I've had guys shower me with compliments, send me flowers, one even wrote me a poem."

Dylan's eyes widened, and she could almost see the thought "*Shit, I should've written a poem,*" run past his eyes. Lucy shook her head. "Thing was, they weren't doing it to make me happy. They were doing it in the hope that I'd make them happy. You get me like no one ever has. I don't know how, since we're so different. But I don't care that we're different. I've missed you the last few days…" Her voice faltered, and she had to swallow against tears rising to the surface. "More than I thought I would. It, *us*, probably won't be easy, but good things usually aren't. So, if you're asking, then I'm saying yes."

He pulled her fingers away from his lips. "I'm asking."

Her lower lip trembled, but she was so happy, she was about to burst. "Then, yes."

"That's what I wanted to hear." Still holding her hand, he leaned in for a kiss. When his lips touched hers, it was like sunlight blossomed in her chest. She wrapped her arms around his neck, running her fingers through his hair. This was right. It was.

"Good job, Dylan," Otis said, laughing from behind them. "Oh, sorry. I'm interrupting. And kissing's gross. The end."

He shut the playroom door again, and Lucy pulled away. She shook her head, sighing. "You want to retract your offer? I'm kind of a package deal."

"Otis and I have an understanding. Man to man." Dylan leaned his forehead against hers. "And nothing will make me change my mind. I'm looking forward to the chaos you'll bring to my senior year."

"And I'm looking forward to the order you'll bring to mine."

They went in for another kiss just as the curtain flapped open. Mom squawked and backed out of the workroom. Lucy dropped her head against Dylan's chest. "You want to get out of here?"

"I thought you'd never ask." A wicked smile spread across his face. "We could go swimming."

Laughing, Lucy said, "That's the best idea I've heard all day."

Epilogue

Thanksgiving Break

Dylan held Lucy's hand as they hiked to a little beach at the lake. "It's pretty with all the fall leaves."

"It's the best time of year to come out here. My dad…" She paused, and Dylan's heart ached at the sight of her blinking back tears. "My dad loves to take me out for hikes around Thanksgiving. I wish he was home."

"I can see why he brings you out here. It's nice, and not too cold, either." While she examined some bright orange-red oak leaves, he snuck a quick look at his phone. Still too early. "Let's go sit."

He led her down to the beach and settled down on the log, pulling her into his lap. She ran her fingers through his hair. "I like it longer."

"It's part of my 'go with the flow' makeover plan. No more military haircuts," he said, closing his eyes to enjoy the feel of her fingers digging into his scalp. "Are you sure you're okay with me signing with Texas Tech? That's a long way from here. I won't be able to come home every weekend."

Lucy shifted in his lap. "Five hours *is* a long commute."

"I know. It was the best school with the best scholarship, but I don't like that we'll be long distance." He hated talking about this, but they had to think about it sometime. Lucy had stood proudly with his parents when he signed with Tech and hadn't said a word in protest. Still…it bugged him. How would he function with her so far away?

"Here's the thing." She ran a finger along his cheekbone, raising goose bumps on his arms. "Did you know Tech has a ranked apparel design program?"

Um, what? "No."

"They do. I had no idea, but when they started talking to you, I took a look." She planted a kiss on his cheek and whispered, "I got my acceptance letter before you even signed. Ha!"

He pulled back, mouth open. "You're going to Lubbock?"

"If you don't mind having me around." She reached out to push his jaw closed. "Don't look so surprised. I get some of my dad's GI Bill benefits, so I can afford to go there, and my mom is okay with it. So, why not?"

He laughed. "So you're just going to up and follow me to Lubbock." He leaned in to kiss her. His heart still leapt in surprise that she was his, even after the last several months. "You know, I think I might love you, Lucy Foster."

She kissed him back, smiling against his mouth. "I think I might love you, too, Dylan Dennings. How crazy is that?"

"Good crazy." He was about to kiss her again, and maybe more, when his phone buzzed in his pocket.

Lucy's eyebrow went up. "Is that a text, or are you just happy I love you?"

"Both." He checked the message. "I hate to cut this hike

short, but I have a surprise for you."

"*That* doesn't sound like a line at all." She stood and held out a hand. "'I have a *surprise* for you.'"

When she found out, she was going to laugh a really long time, but he wasn't about to ruin the surprise. "It's totally legit. I promise."

They hiked back out to his car and drove into town to the little diner her family loved so much. They had homemade pecan and chocolate pies and the best fried chicken in town; plus, they bought more of Serena's eggs than anybody in town.

Lucy glanced at him. "Why are we at the Wooden Spoon?"

"I thought we might meet friends for dinner?"

"*That* was the mystery text?" She ran a hand up his arm to his neck as he parked, then leaned over to nip his ear. "Are you *sure* we shouldn't just blow them off?"

Dylan's will was severely tested by that, but he had time to be with her. They had all the time in the world now that she was coming to Lubbock with him. Besides, she wouldn't want to miss this. "Much as I'd like to say yes, not this time."

She sighed dramatically. "Okay, but you're buying me my very own piece of pie. No sharing."

"Deal. Let's go in. They're waiting."

She followed him to the front door. "Who's waiting? This is starting to sound like a spy thriller."

"Take a look."

Dylan opened the door for her, and a tall man in an Army Class B uniform stood. He had gray hair and Lucy's eyes. "Hey there, Punkin.'"

Lucy's knees went weak, and Dylan caught her before she slid to the ground. "Dad?"

He held out his arms. "Happy Thanksgiving."

Then she was laughing and crying as she ran straight into his arms. Colonel Foster kissed her hair, hugging her tight, while Lucy's mom held onto Otis, tears running down her face.

As Dylan backed out of the restaurant to give them time to themselves, Colonel Foster looked over his daughter's head. "Why don't you join us, son?"

It sounded a little like a command, which made sense. The man *was* an officer, and Dylan wanted to impress him. "Yes, sir. I'd like that, sir, if I'm not intruding."

Lucy hiccupped, smiling through her tears. "Oh, I think the two of you are going to get along really well."

Her dad gave Dylan a long stare, then surprised him by smiling, too. "You know what, Punkin'? I think you're right."

Acknowledgments

I'm so thankful for the opportunity to tell stories. When I first started down this path, I wasn't sure a single manuscript I wrote would ever see the light of day, let alone be published. Some of those early works were pretty terrible. So, first, I need to thank the countless critique partners who taught me—with kindness—how to fix broken stories.

Now, I'm so lucky to have an amazing team to help and nurture my work. To the Entangled team, especially my editor Heather Howland, thanks for your continuous support and counsel. Working with y'all is always a joy.

Mr. Querry, your personal writing class, back when I was the tender age of nineteen, taught me that just because one or two people didn't see the value in the pages I read in class didn't mean it wasn't valuable. Even then, I was writing YA, and that was just fine by you.

To my readers—every time one of you writes "swoon!" in a review, a unicorn gets her wings. Or, so my imagination tells me. Y'all are the best!

Finally, I must thank my family. My son, who runs errands

when I'm on deadline. My daughter, who does chores without being asked so I don't have an excuse to leave my desk when I should be working. And my husband, who tells me I can do it, even when I say I can't. Without you, I never would've been able to tackle this journey. You're awesome people, Highley Family!

About the Author

Kendra C. Highley lives in north Texas with her husband and two children. She also serves as staff to four self-important and high-powered cats. This, according to the cats, is her most critical job. She believes in everyday magic, extraordinary love stories, and the restorative powers of dark chocolate.

Discover the **Suttonville Sentinels** *series...*

THE BAD BOY BARGAIN

SWINGING AT LOVE

Also by Kendra C. Highley

FINDING PERFECT

DEFYING GRAVITY

SIDELINED

TIED UP IN YOU
a novel by Erin Fletcher

Everyone says hotshot goalie Luke Jackson is God's gift to girls, but the only girl he *wants* is his best friend, Malina Hall. Problem is, one of his teammates is showing interest, and the guy has more in common with Malina than Jackson ever will. As her best friend, Jackson should get out of the way. But if there's one thing he's learned from hockey, it's to go for what you want, even if it means falling flat on your face. And he's definitely falling for Malina.

ARTIFICIAL SWEETHEARTS
a *North Pole, Minnesota* novel by Julie Hammerle

It's not chemistry between Tinka Foster and Sam Anderson that made them agree to fake date. With her parents trying to set her up with an annoying pro-track golf student, and intentionally single Sam's family pressuring him to find a girlfriend, they could both use a drama-free summer. So it's not his muscular arms and quick wit that makes Tinka suggest they tell everyone they're both taken. Definitely not. And it's not butterflies that makes a kiss for appearances go on way too long. So there's no way fake couldn't be perfect.

Operation Prom Date

a novel by Cindi Madsen

Kate ships tons of fictional couples, but IRL her OTP is her and Mick, the hot quarterback she's crushed on since, like, forever. Since she's flirtationally challenged, she enlists Cooper Callihan, the guy who turned popular seemingly overnight but who used to be a good friend, to help her land Mick in time for prom. Cooper didn't know how addicting spending time with Kate would be, though, or how the more successful the Operation is, the more jealousy he experiences.

Daring the Bad Boy

an *Endless Summer* novel by Monica Murphy

A session at summer camp is just what shy Annie McFarland needs to reinvent herself. Too bad her fear of water keeps her away from the lake, and her new crush Kyle. Enter Jacob Fazio — junior counselor, all-around bad boy, and most importantly: lifeguard. When a night of Truth or Dare gets him roped into teaching Annie how to swim, she begs him to also teach her how to snag Kyle. Late-night swim sessions turn into late-night kissing sessions…but there's more on the line than just their hearts. If they get caught, Jake's headed straight to juvie.